DIRTY OPERATIONS

SPECIAL WEAPONS & TACTICS 3

PEYTON BANKS

CONTENTS

Chapter 1	1
Chapter 2	12
Chapter 3	24
Chapter 4	35
Chapter 5	47
Chapter 6	59
Chapter 7	71
Chapter 8	85
Chapter 9	97
Chapter 10	107
Chapter 11	117
Chapter 12	128
Chapter 13	138
Chapter 14	152
Chapter 15	164
Chapter 16	175
Chapter 17	181
Chapter 18	192
Chapter 19	202
Chapter 20	214
Chapter 21	225
Chapter 22	234
Chapter 23	244
Chapter 24	256
Chapter 25	266
Epilogue	272

A Note From the Author 277
About the Author 279
Also by Peyton Banks 281

Copyright © 2019 by Peyton Banks

Editor: Emmy Ellis with Studioenp.

Cover Design by Studioenp.

This is a work of fiction. Names, characters, organizations, businesses, events, and incidents are a figment of the author's imagination and are used fictitiously. Any similarities to real people, businesses, locations, history, and events are a coincidence.

All rights reserved.

No part of this publication may be reproduced, distributed, or transmitted in any form or by any means, including photocopying, recording, or other electronic or mechanical methods, without the prior written permission of the publisher.

"Being deeply loved by someone gives you strength, while loving someone deeply gives you courage."

--Lao Tzu

1

"Officer Fraser! Officer Fraser!" Faces appeared outside the window of Ash's cruiser.

He grinned, putting the car in park.

"Watch out!" He laughed, waving the excited boys from his car. Pulling out the keys, he opened the door and stepped out.

"You're just in time!" eleven-year-old Lucas Thomas announced.

"You can be the pitcher," his classmate, Chip Dickens, said.

They grabbed his arm and dragged him along.

Ashton Fraser loved his involvement with the community. He was the DARE officer for Caledonia Elementary School. It was located in one of the rough neighborhoods of Columbia. The children in these parts of the city benefited from having positive interactions with the police. He and a few other officers from the district had taken Caledonia under their wing.

"Okay! Okay!" He chuckled, following them across the parking lot. He drew his sunglasses from his cargo pocket and shielded his eyes. The day was perfect for the kids to be out running around. The sun was high, and the temperature was steadily rising. The baseball diamond was located on the other side of the playground.

But today wasn't a day for the good ol' American pastime.

No, it was kickball time.

Thankfully, he was dressed for the game in his CPD t-shirt, shorts, and tennis shoes. Today was the day for him to spend at the school. Most of the students were from low-income families, single-parent homes with no male role model.

Ash was one of the fortunate kids of Columbia who'd grown up in a loving, two-parent home. Larry and Bernice Fraser were going on thirty-five years of wedded bliss. He and his younger sister, Gizzy, hadn't wanted for anything as children. His parents were blue-collar workers and ensured that he and Gizzy were well-rounded and gave back to their community. He'd grown up to be a cop, and Gizzy was a school-teacher in another district.

Ash took in the children running and screaming around on the playground and felt something for them. Today, after school, he had a surprise for the kids. One of the guys from the K9 unit was going to be bringing one of the canine officers to meet them.

"We're going against Ms. Fletcher's class. Miss Dawson told us to make sure we beat them," Chip said, grabbing his arm and tugging as if he were afraid Ash would up and disappear.

Miss Dawson.

Just the mention of the fifth-grade teacher sent Ash's gaze wandering the area in search of her.

Deana Dawson was one of the sexiest elementary school teachers Ash had ever seen. He'd have to admit half of the reason he made sure to show up to the school was because of her.

He glanced over and found her standing near the field speaking with one of the male teachers and, as always, she took his breath away. The curvy, brown-skinned woman had short, reddish ringlets that made his fingers ache to pull on one of the curls. She had on a summer dress, made proper with a sweater and heels.

Jesus, her heels.

He didn't see how she wore those all day dealing with a class full of rambunctious ten- and eleven-year-olds.

But he was glad she did.

Her calves were perfectly displayed, sending a rush of desire to his lower region.

She turned with a wide grin and looked directly at

him. Ash released a silent curse, thankful he had his shades on.

"Miss Dawson, I found Officer Fraser!" Lucas shouted, arriving at her side first. His brown skin glistened from the heat. He was tall for his age, standing a few inches over Miss Dawson.

"No, you didn't! I saw him pull into the parking lot first!" Chip snapped, spinning to Lucas.

The boys glared at each other, ready to argue.

"Okay, boys. Officer Fraser was not lost." She focused her attention on the boys who both calmed down instantly with her perfect smile.

Her sweet southern drawl wasn't lost on Ash. He was a good ol' southern boy and he didn't think his drawl was that thick.

"He comes the same day every week, and I'd think by now he'd know the way."

What he wouldn't give to sit in her class and just hear her teach all day.

He blinked.

Hell, Ash was captivated by Miss Dawson just as the boys were. He was sure every male, young or old, had a crush on Miss Dawson.

"Yes, ma'am," the boys echoed.

"Hello, Officer Fraser." She turned on her megawatt smile, and Ash froze.

His mouth grew dry, and he released a cough.

"Afternoon, Miss Dawson. Beautiful day," he said, finally able to get words to form.

"That it is. I hope you are ready for kickball. The kids have been dying for you to get here."

"I wouldn't miss it for the world." He tousled Chip's hair. The way his heart was racing reminded him of how he felt once he and his SWAT team finished a call.

The adrenaline wore off, and his body went haywire.

"Go grab Officer Fraser a ball so he can pitch," she instructed.

The boys raced off in search of the ball that would be used for the game.

"You aren't joining us?" he joked, raising his eyebrows.

"Me?" she scoffed. "I wouldn't want to show off my skills and make you all feel worthless on the field."

A grin spread across his face. "Is that a challenge, Miss Dawson?"

The kids waiting near them paused their conversations and listened.

"Miss Dawson, you never play with us!" Chip noted, walking over. He tossed the kickball to Ash.

He caught it with one hand and faced her again, tucking the ball against his hip.

"Yes, Miss Dawson. Why don't you play?" a young

girl named Sara asked, coming to stand next to Miss Dawson.

"I'm not dressed to play," Miss Dawson answered with a laugh.

"But Officer Fraser comes every week on the same day. Next week you can wear regular clothes and play," Lucas said.

"Yes, Miss Dawson, I'm here on the same day every week as you pointed out before," Ash chimed in.

Her eyes narrowed on him, and he instantly felt a tightening below his belt. He groaned internally, knowing this wasn't the time for his cock to wake up. He surely didn't want to direct this conversation into anything near the birds and the bees to explain the tenting in his shorts. "Who wants Miss Dawson to play with us next week?" he asked, turning to the kids. He knew it was a dirty trick to get the children involved, but at this point, he was desperate.

Every hand went up.

"I'll get in on that game!" Ms. Fletcher called out, jogging over with her hand raised.

The kids grew excited by the announcement.

"Come on, Miss Dawson, what do you have to lose?"

Ash spun to Miss Dawson who tilted her chin up in the air. Her gaze cut to him, and he had to fight not to adjust himself.

"You all want me to play kickball." She paused and looked around at everyone surrounding them.

The kids begged and pleaded with their wide grins and hopeful eyes. Ash had to keep himself from joining them. He would love to see Miss Dawson in shorts and t-shirt. Hell, he'd love to see her in less.

She barked a laugh and shook her head. "Then next week, it's on."

The kids cheered pulling Ash out onto the field. He glanced back and caught her staring at him. If her eyes could kill, he'd be pushing up daisies.

At the moment, it would be totally worth it.

"He's so into you," Erin murmured, elbowing Deana.

Erin Fletcher was a close friend. They'd worked together for the last five years and had grown close. They both taught fifth grade and always had their classrooms compete against each other.

Didn't matter what it was.

Kickball, which class could read the most books in a semester, fifth-grade Jeopardy, the list grew longer each year.

Their competitions were legendary.

The kids couldn't wait to get to the fifth grade because they knew Miss Fletcher and Miss Dawson were two teachers who took the time to ensure their classes had fun while learning.

Deana had to tear her gaze from the field. She was captivated by Officer Fraser. Her heart raced while she watched him with the kids.

He gave one of the other boys a high five, and her ovaries did a little dance.

Get a grip.

She blew out a deep breath. She leaned on the fence and adjusted her sweater. Her breasts were traitors, pressing against her dress.

Officer Fraser was dressed in a dark t-shirt that molded along his chest, displaying his rippling muscles. The tattoos on his forearms had her wanting to explore them.

She didn't know when tattooed forearms became sexy, but on him, it was downright erotic.

He was in top shape. He had to be. Since he'd started working with their school for the DARE program, she'd learned a little more about him. He was a cop for Columbia and was SWAT.

Jesus.

She read romance novels and watched television shows, and every single one of them that depicted a SWAT officer was alpha and knew how to take charge, but none of them could hold a candle to the real-life SWAT officer out on the mound.

"I don't know what you are talking about," Deana replied, turning toward her friend. She hoped her eyes gave an innocent appearance, because deep down, Deana knew there was interest from the hot cop.

But he hadn't made a move yet.

Deana was frustrated. He'd been coming to the school for about a year now and he'd yet to make a move.

Maybe it was just harmless flirting and she was reading too much into it.

"You do know what I'm talking about." Erin rolled her eyes. She pushed her glasses on top of her head and focused on Deana. "Every woman with a pulse would die for a chance with the hot cop. Even Mrs. Runion."

"She's like sixty-two and married." Deana giggled.

Kathy Runion was a short, plump, grandmotherly woman. She taught sixth grade and had recently celebrated her fortieth wedding anniversary with her husband, Chuck.

"I said every woman with a pulse." Erin snorted. "We all lost the chance for his attention the minute he saw you."

"Well, if that's the case, why hasn't he like, um, made a move?"

"Who said he had to be the one to make the first move?" Erin cocked an eyebrow. "Why don't you ask him out? This is the twenty-first century. Women are more independent."

Deana gulped at the thought.

There was no way she could do that. She was a southern gal and had always been taught the man should make the first move. She refused to believe chivalry was dead. Her mother would read her the riot act if she found out Deana had asked a man out on a date.

Hell, she'd never done it before.

Didn't even know how to go about it.

Did one just walk up and say, *Hey. I think you're hot. Why don't you take me out on a date?*

Deana turned back to the game and observed Officer Fraser roll the ball for Lucas. He ran toward the ball and kicked it hard.

The ball flew up in the air and over the far fence. The kids screamed and celebrated.

"Home run! Go, Lucas!" Deana hollered. She jumped up and down, watching him run around the bases.

Deana was competitive in nature. She was the youngest of three kids and was used to having to compete against her siblings. Her brother, Karver, was the oldest, and her sister, Yanni, was a couple of years older than her.

Deana faced Erin and stuck her tongue out.

"That's okay. We'll see who is celebrating next week out on the field," Erin threatened, wagging a finger at Deana.

The bell rang, signaling the end of recess.

"Bring it." Deana laughed, holding her hands out. She walked backwards and did a little dance, taunting her friend.

The kids ran past toward the building, giggling at her.

Her eyes met those of Officer Ashton Frasier, and her breath caught her throat. He stood speaking with a few kids in the field. His crooked grin made her heart skip a beat.

This was her chance.

She tossed him a wink, and his grin widened. She twirled around and began walking back to the school. She put a little more emphasis on the sway of her hips, feeling the heat of his gaze on her. Her heels clicked along the pavement, and she picked up her pace.

It may not have been as drastic as Erin had recommended.

But Deana Dawson had just made her move.

2

Loud rock music pumped through the speakers. Trails of sweat slid along Ash's temples. He grunted and pushed the bar up in the air.

"There you go. Give me another one," Myles ordered.

Ash breathed through the rep and pushed harder. His muscles strained as he did another one. It was early Saturday morning, and they were on call for the day.

All week, his mind had been replaying the wink Deana had directed to him. It was the first time she'd purposely flirted with him. When she'd turned and walked away, he'd known immediately she was putting that extra sway in her hips for him. His gaze had been locked on her ass.

He'd almost forgotten he had been talking with his DARE kids and nearly chased after her.

He blew out through his gritted teeth, feeling the

burn in his muscles. His arms automatically rose and fell. His motions slowed.

Today Myles was trying to kill him.

He was sure of it.

His friend and fellow SWAT team member jokingly added more weights to the bar, professing today they needed to take their workout to the next level.

"Son of a bitch," he growled, holding the bar up in the air.

"Stop your whining, Fraser." Myles moved closer, holding his hands near the bar.

"Fuck!" His arms fell to his chest and paused. He narrowed his eyes on Myles.

He'd kill his friend.

Make it look like an accident.

"Breathe," Myles instructed.

Ash inhaled sharply.

Myles carefully watched Ash, making sure the bar didn't fall. "Come on. You got this. One more."

Ash gritted his teeth and pushed the bar up and, with Myles help, set it in the cradle. He sat up, out of breath. He barely caught the water bottle Myles tossed to him. His arms felt like loose noodles after this workout.

He opened the bottle and took a few gulps. His gaze took in the department's weight room. It had gone over a massive upgrade a few years ago. The captain was able to get some donations to renovate the gym. There were quite a few people spread throughout the gym working out. A few women were on the ellipticals while one of the beat cops was running on a treadmill.

It was a popular spot for many to blow off steam.

It had been much needed, and now they had state-of-the-art equipment so the police force could stay in shape without having to go to local places.

"Any plans this weekend?" he asked, finally able to catch his breath. He stood, rotating to Myles.

"Nah. This is the first weekend I don't have anything planned in a long while. Me and my couch will be getting reacquainted."

"Sounds good to me. As long as everything remains quiet, we should have a good weekend," Ash said. He grabbed his towel and wiped off the bench so Myles could take his turn.

"Don't be fucking jinxing us." Myles snorted, taking his seat.

Ash chuckled and threw the towel down on the floor. "You sure it won't be you and Miss Righty this weekend?" He jerked his right hand and wagged his eyebrows.

"Fuck you." Myles rolled his eyes and laid down on the bench. "Get over here and spot me."

Ash ambled over and stood behind the bench.

Myles grabbed the bar and did the first set. He was focused while he benched the weights.

"Not as easy as it seems?" Ash taunted, chuckling as he noticed his friend was already slowing down. Myles had only been too happy to let Ash go first. He knew without a doubt he may be sore tomorrow.

"You're an ass," Myles replied through gritted teeth. He pushed the bar in the air and paused.

"You good?" Ash stepped closer and held his hands out, prepared to grab the bar if need be.

"Yeah. Can't let you show me up," Myles growled. He did a few more reps before settling the bar down in the cradle. He jumped up from the bench, flexing his arms.

Ash caught a few of the women whispering and staring in their direction while they both wiped down with towels. His gaze flickered over to them, and he wasn't interested. He reached for his shirt and tossed it onto his shoulder.

Neither of them were a certain teacher that had plagued his mind.

Hell, he wasn't even sure she'd noticed him until she'd thrown the wink.

He officially took that as a challenge.

"How about grabbing a few beers tonight? I'll make sure you are back in time to get home to Miss Righty." He dodged Myles's towel with a laugh.

"Well, look who's here. They just let anyone in this place," a deep voice sounded from behind him.

Ash turned, a wide grin spread across his face. Walking toward them was Zain and Iker.

"Tweedle Dee and Tweedle Dum," Ash smiled, moving toward his other teammates.

They shook hands and pounded each other on the backs in greeting.

Zain and Iker had joined SWAT around the same time Ashton had. The three of them were the only members of their SWAT unit who had not served in the military. Myles and Brodie had been Special Forces, while their two sergeants, Mac and Declan, had been SEALs.

"What are you two ugly fuckers getting into tonight?" Zain asked, crossing his arms in front of his chest.

"I was trying to talk Myles into going out tonight," Ash said.

"I hear the fight is going to be on down at the Pub," Iker announced. "We can snag a table, watch the fight, and drink away."

"Fight and a beer is right up my alley." Ash nodded. "Come on, Grandpa. What you say?" he asked, turning to Myles.

"You got a hot date tonight?" Zain asked Myles.

They all focused their attention to him, waiting for a response.

Myles rolled his eyes and let loose a curse.

"You motherfuckers get on my nerves. I wasn't going to be doing shit but chilling on my couch and watching a movie tonight," Myles snapped.

"There'll be plenty of time for that later. I'll call Brodie and see what he's up to," Iker offered. "I'm sure Mac and Dec are both too busy becoming homebodies now."

"I'd like to see you say that to either of their faces." Myles snickered.

They all chuckled knowing none of them had the balls to.

"We'll see ya there," Ash said, grabbing Myles by the shoulders and directing him to the locker room.

There was nothing better than hanging with his brothers, drinking and watching a good old fight.

***

"Erin, I'm not sure about this," Deana grumbled.

Her friend just couldn't leave her alone. Erin paralleled parked her car and shut the engine off before turning toward Deana.

Just because she was twenty-eight and single, it did

not mean she had to spend her time at a bar on a Saturday night. She was satisfied with curling up on her couch with her blanket, a bottle of wine, and a steamy romance book.

"You sound like my grandmother." Erin sighed drastically. "You know what, I'll take that back. GiGi goes out way more than you. Hell, I can't keep up with that eighty-year-old's schedule."

"Bars are just not my thing." Deana sniffed.

It was pointless.

Erin Fletcher was determined to get her tipsy and have fun.

How dare she.

"Come on. We'll go in, sit at the bar, have a few drinks, flirt, and then we'll leave. Harmless fun." Erin exited her car and slammed the door shut.

Deana blew out a deep breath, hoisted her purse up on her shoulder, and joined her on the sidewalk. She wiped her sweaty hands on her leggings and willed her nervousness away.

"You can at least act as if you are ready to have some fun. You look like you are going to be executed." Erin danced in place.

Deana smiled at her friend.

"We are not going to waste these sexy outfits for nothing."

Maybe she should relax. She was twenty-eight, had a career, and had a beautiful home.

She had made a good life for herself.

"Okay." Deana laughed. "Let's have some fun."

Erin squealed and entwined her arm with Deana's.

"You will have fun. I promise," she said, leading the way. It was a warm night. The street was crowded with people out to enjoy the nightlife in downtown Columbia. "Hell, maybe you might meet Mr. Right tonight."

"Erin." Deana groaned.

"I got to thinking. You're right. If the hot cop hasn't said anything by now, he must be stupid. How could he not want you?"

"Erin. It's okay." She tried to smile but failed miserably at it.

Even after her wink and sexy walk away from him, he hadn't even approached her after school. She had seen him before she had left for the day. He'd been out in the parking lot with the K9 unit. The kids were so excited to be able to watch the cops' demonstration with the K9 officer.

She blew out a deep breath.

Maybe she did need to start living a little.

He must not be interested.

"I say we look for some hot guys. The fight is on, and I'm sure there will be plenty of them out tonight."

They arrived at the bar and entered the establishment. It was crowded, and they beelined it straight to the bar. Thankfully, there were two seats left, and they were able to claim them before someone else did.

Deana glanced around the bar and took in the crowd. Televisions were scattered around with tables near them. Each chair had a body in it as everyone waited for the fight to come on. The atmosphere was electric. Music blared from the speakers.

There was a pool table and even a small dance floor where some partiers were trying to show off their moves.

Deana relaxed. Tonight, she would do as her friend had begged.

Have fun.

"What can I get you, pretty ladies?"

Deana turned to find the bartender smiling at them. He was dressed like most of the staff in dark t-shirt and jeans. He could be considered handsome, but he just didn't do anything for Deana.

"I'll have an Old Fashioned, please," Deana replied with a smile.

"Oh, I have the same!" Erin laughed.

He nodded and walked away to make their drinks. The bar was busy, and since they'd arrived, it seemed as if more people had come in.

They began chatting about everything and then some. Deana couldn't remember the last time she'd just let loose. The pre-show was on for the fight. Anticipation was growing because the two opponents were popular and had been trash-talking for the past few months. The crowd was thick, and all were in a good mood.

After the second round of drinks, Deana knew she'd have to slow down. She hadn't really been a hard drinker, and most of her days of having fun in a bar had been back in college.

"So, I have to come clean," Erin announced. Her wide eyes were glossy, and there was a twinkle in them that made Deana groan.

"What have you done?" Deana leaned against the counter, staring at her friend.

"Remember that guy I had been talking to?" she asked, tucking her hair behind her ear. Erin bit her lip and stared at Deana, trying to look innocent.

"Jerry or Jim—"

"Jenson." Erin laughed.

Deana nodded. Her friend had met this guy online, and they had been casually talking on the phone.

"Well, he wanted to meet, and I kind of texted him that I'd be here tonight."

"Well, why'd you bring me?" Deana asked.

"Because it will be the first time we'd be meeting, and I wanted it in a public place and have you with me."

That was a smart idea. A woman couldn't be too safe nowadays.

"Well, why didn't you just say so?" She shrugged. She didn't mind chaperoning so to speak. Erin was a beautiful girl, and any guy who caught her would be lucky.

"Well, that was the easy part."

Deana froze and glared at her friend. "What is that supposed to mean?"

"He's bringing his friend."

"Erin!" Deana huffed and rolled her eyes.

"Please, Deana. It's just hanging out. Not a date. We won't be separated at all. I promise."

Erin gave her the best puppy-dog look that even Deana couldn't stay mad at. She laughed and shook her head.

"Fine. But this is not a date, and nor will there be any future ones with the friend."

Erin squealed and wrapped her arms around Deana in a tight hug. "You won't be sorry. I'm just so happy to finally meet him, and then you can, too!"

Deana signaled for the bartender and asked for a water. She wanted to pace herself and didn't want to chance getting too tipsy. Someone had to remain sober tonight.

"Oh, there he is, and the friend doesn't appear half bad."

Deana turned in the direction Erin was pointing and noticed two men walking their way. The first one, tall with dark-brown hair, waved and smiled at Erin. His friend was average in the looks department, tall and fit. Deana shrugged and put on a smile.

3

"You boys up for another round?" the waitress asked. She cocked her eyebrow and placed her hand on her hips. Her long blonde hair hung past her shoulders. She was on the thin side with her low-cut dark t-shirt putting her cleavage on display.

Her gaze circulated around the table, and Ash was certain she licked her lips. Interest was definitely on her face, and he had a feeling she would be leaving with whoever made the offer first.

"Hell yeah! On me this time!" Ash shouted, raising his hand.

The guys lifted their glasses and cheered. The waitress, Cindy...Candy...Sheila, whatever the hell her name was, nodded and smiled. She turned and disappeared into the crowd.

"Who's taking the bait?" Zain chuckled, cocking his thumb in the direction she'd disappeared.

"What? The waitress?" Iker asked, downing the last of his beer.

"Too skinny." Ash shook his head. Thoughts of someone he wanted to take home came to mind. A short, honey-brown-skinned teacher who had an infatuation with heels.

"Our boy is right. I need someone thick I don't have to worry about breaking," Myles joked, flexing his arms, showcasing his muscles. Myles was a tall black man who exuded confidence. He, like the rest of the men around the table, was in top physical shape and took pride in their appearance.

Female cheers broke through the air.

Their attention whipped over to a table full of women who were making no attempt to hide the fact they had their eyes on Ash and his brothers.

Myles pointed to one of the women and winked. Ash barked a laugh as she pretended to faint into her friend.

He loved times like this. These men were his brothers. He would do anything for each of them. They trained together, worked together, and loved partying together.

Their waitress returned with their drinks. They released a cheer to greet her, helping her pass out the cold, frothy mugs. Ash grabbed his mug and brought it to his mouth. The crowd blocking the bar parted, and his hand froze. His attention landed on a familiar figure standing at the bar.

Deana. Fucking. Dawson.

His gaze raked over her body, and he about swallowed his tongue. She had on a shirt that slid off her shoulder, showcasing her smooth skin. Her legs were encased in leather leggings that displayed her thick hips and calves. His focus dropped down to her heels.

Those fucking heels.

Ash's gaze whipped to the man who was standing next to her smiling and speaking in her ear over the loud music. He took notice of the other teacher, her friend, Erin Fletcher, waving for Deana and the guy to follow her and her date. His eyes trailed the four as they moved over to the pool table.

Shit.

He sipped the beer, no longer tasting it. His buzz was gone. He was too busy watching the guys rack up the balls on the table while Deana and Erin spoke quietly together.

Alarms went off in the back of his head. He was good at reading people, and he zeroed in on the way Deana stood. As a member of SWAT, it was his job. He was the team's negotiator and was damn good at noticing body language.

Deana's was guarded.

Miss Fletcher was laughing and talking, and Deana

was smiling, but it didn't reach her eyes. Her head turned, and their gazes met.

Ash tipped his head up in a nod.

She smiled and gave him a short wave. Erin twisted around before dismissing him.

"Who is that?" Myles asked, leaning over to check out who Ash had been watching.

"One of the teachers from Caledonia," he replied. He took another long gulp of his beer then set it down. "Deana Dawson."

"That's the one you were thinking of asking out?" Myles cocked an eyebrow and gave a low whistle. He shoved Ash slightly. "What is there to think about? She's fine."

His gaze flickered back over to the pool table and found the guy standing next to Deana. Ash watched her glance up and offered the man a small smile.

Looked like he may have missed his chance with the teacher.

Ash released a curse and tossed back the rest of his beer. He signaled for another drink. This one needed to be stronger.

A hell of a lot stronger.

Something to make him feel numb for missing the opportunity with Deana.

"Yeah, well, there's nothing to think about now," he muttered, dragging his attention away from Deana.

The pre-show for the fight was finally over, and the packed bar was getting restless waiting for the main event.

Ash sat back, no longer in the mood to party. He couldn't help thinking about Deana. He tried to glance back over in her direction, but the crowd had shifted, blocking his view.

He released a curse.

Brodie said something that was lost on Ash, but the guys around the table fell out into a fit of laughter. He tried to focus back on his brothers but failed.

"Here ya go, honey," the waitress said, setting his glass down in front of him.

Ash's gaze dropped down to her name tag.

Tiffany.

"Thanks, Tiff," he murmured, grabbing the large shot glass.

"Anytime, suga." She winked and moved around the table, dropping off and picking up mugs and glasses.

"Anyone call Mac and Dec to invite them out?" Zain asked, raising his eyebrow.

Ash knew he hadn't called. He'd figured someone would. He looked around the table. There were guilty expressions on everyone's faces.

Shit.

Mac was going to have all their balls, and Dec

would probably take them and shove them up their asses.

The crowd parted again, revealing the area where Deana was with her friend and those assholes.

He wasn't sure when her date had become an asshole.

Probably back on his fourth beer.

For all Ash knew, he was a great guy, but since he was on a date with the object of Ash's desire, the guy had been upgraded to asshole.

His annoyance flared that he hadn't approached her the other day. Her wink and the sight of her hips swaying had left him hard for hours. He gripped the glass tight, trying not to crush it in his hand.

He knocked the drink back, and the clear liquid burned its way down his throat. He winced and blinked. His gaze landed on Deana, and he paused.

Something was off.

The way she stood and glared at the guy had Ash slowly lowering his glass to the table. There was no signs of her friend and the other guy.

He read her lips and stood from the table with clenched fists.

Stop.

He ignored his name being called and stalked toward her.

"I just want to have fun tonight, baby," Gus said, reaching for her.

She snatched her hand back, silently cursing. Erin and her date, Jenson, had left to go get another round of drinks.

"I don't," she said, hoping her voice remained steady. This asshole just wasn't listening to her. Just because Erin and Jensen were getting close, didn't mean she was ready to just let him have his way with her.

At first, Gus had appeared to be a nice guy, but as the night had gone on, he was becoming real handsy and a jerk.

"Everything about this outfit of yours is saying otherwise," he stated. His smile disappeared, and he narrowed his gaze on Deana.

She backed away from him with a shake of her head. He stepped forward, trapping her into a corner. He gripped her arm and pulled. She resisted, but he held on tight, and she winced.

"I said no." She attempted to pull free, but his hand tightened on her. She bit her lip to keep from crying out. His fingers dug into her forearm as she tried to yank her arm back.

Fear twisted in her gut. What if he dragged her out

of here? No one was paying them attention, and with the bar as packed as it was, there was no telling how long before Erin returned.

"Listen here, bitch—"

"I think you may need to get your hearing checked. The woman said no," a deep voice growled behind Gus.

Gus stiffened and glanced over his shoulder. "This don't have nothing to do with you, pal."

Deana knew that voice, but she'd never heard it with such force and fury. Gone was the playful, deep baritone she was familiar with. She swallowed hard and leaned to the side and was met with the stone-hard face of Ashton Fraser.

"It does when a woman says no and you're not obeying her wishes." His tone was low, but Deana heard it over the crowd cheering. Now that the fight had started, the music had been lowered.

"Listen here, buddy. Why don't you move on. This doesn't have anything to do with you." Gus snickered, turning to Ash but not letting her go.

Ash's gaze dropped down to Gus's grip on her arm, and his jaw tightened.

"Let her go," Ashton snarled. His laser focus settled on Gus. "Before I make you."

"Yeah? You and what army?"

Deana's eyes widened as four large men slowly

filed in behind Ash. Their faces were rigid and deadly. She recognized them as the men he'd been sitting down drinking with. They had to be cops, too. Each of them were tall, muscular, and deserved to be on one of those calendars she always saw floating around on the internet.

She swallowed and glanced up at Gus.

If looks could kill, Gus would be six feet deep.

The color drained from his face. He peered around at the five large men standing before him.

"Hey, Ash. Seems like this motherfucker don't know how to treat a woman," the large black man standing next to Ashton said. He crossed his arms over his massive chest and glared at Gus.

"I'm in the mood to teach tonight," the guy on the other side of Ash announced. His attention was on Gus as well.

Deana's heart raced; she sensed the shit was about to hit the fan.

Gus's grip loosened. Deana pulled free and stepped away from him.

She glanced around and saw every eye was on them. She swallowed hard and rubbed the sore area on her forearm.

"What? Am I supposed to be scared of you?" Gus growled, stepping toward Ashton who had about a couple of inches on him and at least thirty pounds of muscle.

Was he that drunk? Or was he really that crazy?

"What is going on?" Erin appeared by her side with Jensen in tow.

"Gus, what the fuck?" Jensen snapped, setting the drinks on the pool table. He eyed the five men standing in front of his friend and moved next to Gus. "What the fuck have you done?"

"Not a damn thing." Gus's chuckle sent a chill down Deana's spine. "We were just about to have a good time, and these fuckers came over here."

Obviously seeing Deana rub her skin, Erin moved closer, examining her arm. "Are you all right? Did he hurt you?"

Deana's gaze flickered to Ashton. His nostrils flared, and he took a step toward Gus.

"Apologize," he growled. His hands closed into tight fists, and the fury that rolled onto his face wasn't lost on Deana.

Gus barked a laugh and pushed Jensen out the way. "Or what?"

Wrong response.

Ashton pulled back his fist and slammed it into Gus's face. The bar flew into a frenzy. Deana was shoved out of the way as the brawl ensued between Ashton and Gus.

It was a mismatched fight from the start.

Ashton was easily overpowering Gus. Fist were thrown, and grunts could be heard.

Deana and Erin were shoved farther away from the fight. Security pushed past them to try to break up the melee.

Terror overtook Deana as she lost sight of Ashton.

4

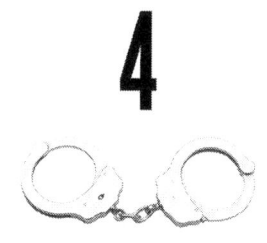

"Come on. This way," Erin shouted.

Deana swallowed hard and let Erin guide her out of the way. She turned back one last time to try to get a glimpse of Ashton. The throng of people in that area was thick, preventing her.

They followed the crowd out the front door.

Deana breathed a sigh of relief. The sounds of sirens grew louder. She turned. Four black-and-white patrol cars flew up and halted. The cops jumped out and stalked to the bar. The crowd stood around waiting out in the street and on the sidewalk.

"What happened?" Erin asked, wrapping her arm around Deana.

"To be honest, I'm still trying to process. One minute, he was cool. It was like the second you and Jensen left, he flipped," she replied. She bit her lip to keep it from trembling.

"I'm so sorry. I shouldn't have left." Erin rubbed a hand along her back.

The motion comforted Deana a little, but she was fine.

Away from the jerk.

She was worried about Ashton. She hoped he wouldn't be punished for fighting. The news always had stories of cops being arrested while off duty, and she wished he wasn't one of them trying to defend her.

"You didn't know. Hell, I didn't see it coming. He kept trying to touch me and convince me to kiss him. I didn't want to, and he wasn't taking no for an answer."

"How did Officer Fraser get over there?"

"I have no clue. But I'm so thankful that he did." She moved away from her friend, watching the police drag a handcuffed Gus out the door.

He tried to resist, shouting the entire way.

Deana shook her head in complete disbelief at the outcome of the night.

Her attention was drawn to the door as Ash exited with a few of the cops. She took him all in and noticed he didn't have handcuffs on.

He stopped and spoke with the uniformed cops while his friends strolled out of the bar as if nothing had happened.

"Let me take you home," Erin said.

"I didn't mean to ruin your date—"

'Hey, don't worry about it. If that is the type of scum Jensen hangs out with, I'm done." She shook her head. "I don't need that type of drama. No, thanks."

Deana realized she'd lost her purse in the scuffle. "Oh no! I'm going to have to go back in there. I lost my purse."

"Okay. Let's see if they will let us reenter."

Deana turned back and met the gaze of Ashton. His gaze traveled the length of her body, and her gut clenched. Her heart skipped a beat as she got closer to him.

He moved away from the cop he was speaking with and made his way to her.

"Deana, are you okay?" he asked, his eyes boring into hers.

She swallowed hard, her mouth going dry. Whenever they were around each other at the school, he'd always called her Miss Dawson. Hearing him call her by her first name weakened her knees.

"Yeah, I'm fine. Just shook up," she breathed.

He seemed to relax at her words.

She took in a slight shadowing on his cheek and a small cut over his eye. "You're hurt." She reached up and immediately touched the area with her finger.

"This?" He chuckled.

Her core clenched at the sound of his laughter. His devilishly sexy lips spread into a wide grin.

He gripped her hand in his and entwined their fingers. "This is nothing. I get worse in training."

"You think they'll let us back in there? She lost her purse," Erin's voice broke through Deana's erotic train of thought.

Her heart raced with the feel of his large hand around hers.

"Yo, Ash! Here's her purse." The large black man that had stood next to Ashton was walking to them with her purse in his hands.

"Thank you," she exhaled, taking it from him.

Ashton's hand tightened on hers when she tried to pull away.

"Sorry for going through it. Saw your license and didn't want the beat cops to try to put it in evidence or something." He shrugged.

"Deana, this is my partner, Myles Burton. Myles, this is Deana Dawson and her friend, Erin Fletcher," Ash said, making introductions.

Deana gave a tight smile and took Myles's hand, as did Erin.

"We need to go, Deana. It's getting late, and this is too much, even for me." Erin laughed, waving her hand at the circus around them. The crowd was still thick and was probably hoping to get back into the bar since the ruckus was now under control. "I'll take you home."

"I'll take her," Ash said, pulling her to his side.

Erin's eyebrows shot up. Deana glanced at him before turning to Erin.

It didn't take long for her to make up her mind.

"I'm going to go with him." Deana nodded. He had just fought a guy for her. She could at least let him escort her home.

"Okay." Erin smiled and had a twinkle in her eye.

Deana resisted the urge to roll her eyes. Her friend was reading too much into his offer to take her home.

"Pretty lady, I'll escort you to your car," Myles offered.

"Why thank you." Erin turned and began walking away with Myles.

Deana caught Erin's glance and the wink thrown at her. She shook her head as her friend entwined her arm with Myles.

"So, you're a cop too, huh?" Erin said.

Deana glanced down at their still entwined hands before looking up.

"Come on, Miss Dawson. Let's get you home."

Ash pulled her through the throng. They continued walking down the street away from the bar. They sauntered across to a parking lot.

They didn't say a word. Ashton had yet to release her hand. The click of her heels echoed around them.

Arriving at his car, she turned to him once he'd opened the passenger door.

"Ashton," she began.

"Ash," he murmured, standing close to her.

She cocked her head back so she could meet his gaze.

He reached up with his free hand and trailed his fingers along the side of her temples and down to her cheek. "Say it."

"Ash," she breathed. Her knees grew weak, and she leaned into him. Her core clenched at his hardness. "Thank you. You didn't have to come to my rescue."

"I did. What kind of man would I be to let that jerk lay his hands on you? I'm pissed I didn't get over there quicker." He blew out a deep breath and glanced away before turning his attention back to her. "But it should have been me."

"What?" she asked, confused.

"It should have been me you were out on a date with."

"That wasn't a date." She shook her head. His confused look made her quickly explain what Erin had set up.

"Still. Had I asked you out, you wouldn't have been in that situation."

Deana's cheeks warmed. She glanced down and gasped. She let his hand go and reached for the other one. She brought it up, and even in the low illumination from the streetlight, she could see the bruises and busted knuckles.

"You are hurt," she exclaimed and gently ran her fingers along his red knuckles. Dried blood was scattered on his hand.

"I'll be fine. Come on, pretty lady. Let's get you home."

Ash pulled into Deana's driveway and cut the engine. He turned to her and took her in.

Everything about Deana Dawson had him tied up in knots. She was smart and sexy all rolled up in one small package.

They stared at each other before her giggles escaped, breaking up the tension. Ash found himself smiling. Tiredly, he ran a hand along his face.

He had told Deana he was fine, but his hand hurt like a bitch. Just thinking of the way that asshat had gripped her arm had him wanting to beat him down again.

He had seen red when the guy had started spouting off at the mouth and refused to apologize for touching Deana. Before he knew it, his fist had slammed into the guy's face.

He'd do it again.

And again.

He didn't even need his brothers. Ash could have taken on both the guys with Erin and Deana.

The other guy at least had been smart enough to not jump in the middle of things. For that brief moment he had tried to save his friend, but the ass, Gus, apparently thought he was the shit.

Ash had no problem proving to him that he was the bigger man.

"What's so funny?" he asked.

"Us." She leaned back and bit her lip.

His gaze dropped down to that luscious lip, and he ached to be the one to nip it.

"I've been waiting for you to make the first move. It took you fighting another man over me to bring us to this point." She waved her hands around.

"I was waiting on the perfect timing." He exited the car and shut the door. The heat of her shocked gaze followed his movements. He arrived at her door and opened it. Reaching out his hand, he helped her from the car.

Not wanting to let her go, he entwined their fingers together, and they walked silently up her front steps and onto her porch.

She lived in a cute house that looked as if it were

perfect for her. The flowerbeds were perfectly manicured, and the yard was small and well-kept.

"So here we are," she murmured, turning to him.

"Here we are," he echoed.

She reached down and gripped his injured hand and stared at it.

"I can wash this off and bandage it up for you if you like," she offered.

"I'm good. I'll take care of it when I get home." He shook his head, captivated by her lips.

He stepped closer to her, narrowing the gap between them. He reached out and tipped her chin up. Her lips parted slightly with a slight gasp escaping them.

"Deana," he murmured, running a finger along her plump lip.

"Ash," she whispered, leaning into his embrace.

Hearing the sound of his name on her lips ignited a deep passion within his chest. He bent forward and captured her lips with his.

Her soft lips parted, granting him entrance. He swept his tongue in and explored. A hint of bourbon greeted him. Deana's small fingers gripped his t-shirt while he deepened the kiss and captured her moans.

He wrapped his arms around her waist, settling his hands on the curve of her ass. He pressed her closer to him, pushing his hardened length into her abdomen.

Her hands slid up his chest and rested at the base of his neck. Her fingers dove into his hair, gripping it tight as her body molded to his.

Her tongue shyly dueled with his before growing more urgent. His cock strained against his jeans, and he made no qualms about hiding it.

A sexy noise escaped her lips, and it fueled Ash's desire for her. Her ass filled his large hands perfectly, as if made for him.

If he didn't rein it in, he'd be pushing her up against her door and sliding home.

Do it, a voice whispered in his head.

That was not how he'd been raised to treat a lady, and Deana was definitely a lady.

Fuck.

"Deana," he said, tearing his mouth from hers. He gazed down at her swollen lips and flushed cheeks.

Her eyes slowly opened, and he was met with a heated gaze that almost brought him to his knees.

She blinked a few times then her eyes focused on him.

"Did I do something wrong?" she asked. Her hands slid down and rested on his chest.

"What? No." He shook his head, reached up, and ran his thumb along her bottom lip, gritting his teeth for what he was about to do. "Where's your keys?"

Deana stepped back and fumbled around in her

purse, pulling out a keychain. She spun with a small smile spreading on her lips, slid the key into the lock, and turned, opening the door slightly.

Deana stepped forward and motioned for him, holding on to the door. His gaze took in her curvy frame, and his breath caught in his throat. That bare shoulder was driving him slightly insane.

"Why don't you come in so I can clean your hands?" she asked, biting her lip. Her voice was just a hair's breadth above a whisper, and her wide eyes met his while she waited for his response.

Hell, he'd practically forgotten all about his busted knuckles once his lips had covered hers.

He bit back a groan and stepped forward. Tipping her chin up, he pressed a chaste kiss to her lips and pulled back.

"If I come inside tonight, I won't be leaving until tomorrow morning." He stepped back away from her. His lips curled in the corners at the frustrated look that washed over her face.

He was serious.

If he took one step into her home, he wouldn't be able to control himself with her.

He'd pined after her for so long that he had to put some space between them. She was a good woman who deserved to be wooed.

"Lock the door when you close it."

"But, Ash—"

"I'll call you soon." He pushed her inside her house, holding back a laugh at her shocked expression. Her mouth flopped open and closed while she stood frozen in place. "I promise."

He turned and jogged down the stairs without looking back.

If he did, she'd find herself tossed over his shoulder.

Deana Dawson was a woman who deserved to be courted. He was a true southern boy and was up for the challenge.

5

Ash filed into the conference room behind Myles. SWAT had a monthly meeting with leadership. The meetings were generally led by their sergeants, Mac and Declan. It was a bright and early Monday morning, and Ash had yet to have coffee. As soon as this meeting was over, he was going to dash to the break room and look for a cup of the black tar they kept there.

He yawned.

This was the side of being a cop that Ash dreaded. He'd rather be out in the streets patrolling or on a call. Sitting in a stuffy room was restricting, as if the walls were closing in around him.

The conference room was small and had two rows of tables and chairs. At the front was a large television in one corner and a whiteboard dead center. A podium was located at the front for speakers to stand behind.

"Lover boy is here," Zain murmured.

Chuckles floated around.

Brodie, Zain, and Iker were spread out at the tables. Ash could sense all eyes were on him.

Ash snorted, taking his seat in the middle row. Myles grabbed the chair beside him grinning.

"Rescuing damsels in distress," Iker said.

The room filled with laughter.

Ash could take a joke.

He grinned and held up both his hands, flipping his teammate off.

He was feeling the full effects of the brawl. Not that Gus had done much damage. Myles and the others had held the crowd back while Ash had pummeled Gus's face with his fist. It was very satisfying to experience his fist plowing into the asshole's smug face.

He sat back in his chair with a grimace. Ash could have sworn the bouncers had got in a punch or two before they'd pulled him off the asshat.

The skin on his hand had drawn tight. He winced, flexing it open.

Deana was worth it.

"What's with all the noise?" Mac barked, stalking into the room. He marched over to the table in the front.

The laughter immediately ceased. All eyes were on the man behind him.

Captain Spook.

Declan filed in behind the captain and shut the

door. Ash's gaze met his, and he tilted his head in a greeting to his sergeant. Declan made his way over and joined Mac.

Ash released a curse.

Captain Spook was glaring right at him, and he knew he was in for an ass-chewing. The captain was dressed in a dark suit and had yet to knot his tie.

The captain was a tall, commanding man who instantly demanded respect with one look.

The temperature in the room seemed to chill at least ten degrees. Ash sat up in his chair, focused on what the captain had to say.

"This weekend was supposed to be a quiet time spent with the wife." He began walking over to the podium. His steps were steady. He arrived behind the stand and stood with his hands collapsed behind him. His gaze swept the room before landing on Ash.

He swallowed hard.

He knew he was about to get his ass handed to him, but it was all worth it.

"I get a call around one in the morning that men from my precinct were involved in a brawl at a local bar." He paused.

The men shifted uncomfortably. Mac and Declan both turned and eyed the members of SWAT. Declan's gaze landed on Ash. He raised an eyebrow as if to ask what happened. Ash shook his head slightly.

Now was not the time to explain.

"And not just any men," Captain Spook continued. "When I inquired on which of my upstanding officers they were referring to, it would seem members of my SWAT team were involved in an altercation of sorts."

The tension was thick. The silence was palpable. No one dared to make a move. The captain stepped from behind the podium with his hands still collapsed behind him, but anger radiated from his eyes.

"So I had to make a decision. Allow my officer to be arrested, or deal with him myself when he reports to the precinct? My decision was made because he is a damn fine police officer, and I was sure there was a good reason. Wasn't there, Officer Fraser?"

Ash nodded, meeting the captain's glare.

"Yes, sir," he responded, clearing his throat.

Someone let out a curse. All eyes were on him, waiting on an explanation. At the moment, he would rather be facing the barrel of a gun than his captain. He swallowed hard.

Hell, he could be taken off the SWAT team if the captain wanted to. Time to face the music. He'd known this was coming. At the bar, he'd been held up by security while the cops had called his captain. He had figured he would just get summoned into the captain's office, not get reprimanded in front of the team.

But they were all there at the bar except Mac and Declan.

He blew out a deep breath and ran his hand along his jaw.

"We were at the bar for the fight," he began.

Dec and Mac glanced at each other before they returned their attention to him.

He knew a second ass-chewing was going to be coming. "A woman I know was there, one of the teachers from the school where I run the DARE program. She was being harassed by a male."

"I'm assuming the one you were in the altercation with?" Captain Spook interrupted.

Ash nodded. "Yes, sir. He was making advances that she didn't appreciate and he practically had her cornered."

"He's lucky he was able to walk out of the establishment," Myles growled from beside Ash. "His grip on her arm was mighty tight. It took Ash telling him twice to release her before he did."

"Two times too many if you ask me," Brodie chimed in.

Flashes from the other night came to mind. Fear had washed over Deana's face. Something in him had snapped. No woman should be taken advantage of.

Ever.

His men shifted as he continued with the story.

The satisfying crunch of his knuckles meeting cartilage still rang out in his ears.

"Please tell me you broke something on him," Mac growled, his eyes narrowing on Ash.

"Oh, I did," Ash replied.

Mac gave a satisfied grunt and leaned back in his chair.

"Is the guy pressing charges against Ash?" Declan asked, turning to the captain.

"As of now, no." Captain Spook shook his head. "He doesn't have any grounds to stand on. A few people came forward and gave a statement of what they saw between the man and the female. I believe the other precinct is going to speak to the woman and get her side of the story. It would seem Officer Fraser took her home before the patrolmen could speak with her."

"So other people saw the ass harassing her and no one stepped forward?" Myles snarled. He ran his hand along his head before blowing out a deep breath.

Murmurs of disbelief went around.

"Yes, but it would seem Officer Fraser was the only one willing to help. What you did was commendable, Officer Fraser. Just next time don't use your fists. You may not be so lucky next time," Captain Spook said. He stalked to the door and opened it. He paused and turned to face them. "But if I get another call late at night involving any of you in an altercation, you will sit in a jail cell. Do I make myself clear?"

"Yes, sir," they all responded simultaneously.

Captain Spook nodded and glanced over at Mac. "They're all yours."

He disappeared from the room and shut the door behind him. Ash blew out a deep breath.

That could have gone completely differently.

Mac stood and walked over to the podium. He spread some papers out on it before turning his laser-sharp gaze on the team.

"Sergeant Owen, did your phone ring with an invite to go out for drinks and watch the fight?" Mac asked Declan.

Declan pulled his cell from his pocket. He swiped the screen and glanced down at it.

"I don't have any missing calls from any of the team," he drawled. He tossed his phone down on the table before him and leaned back in his chair with his hands collapsed on his head. "Did you?"

Groans filled the air.

"Nope." Mac's voice grew cold. "So let me get this straight. All you fuckers went out for drinks and a fight and didn't think to invite Dec or me?"

"Mac, it was last minute—"

Mac's hard stare cut Zain off. Someone coughed. No one dared to say anything else.

"That's fucked up." Declan's chuckle was low.

Ash cringed.

They had drills coming up, and he knew what that meant.

Hardcore punishment at the hands of their two sergeants.

"Ma'am, next time you are involved in an altercation, please make sure you stay around where the police can speak with you."

"There won't be a next time," Deana snapped. She was irritated that the cop implied she would be involved in another situation such as the one this past weekend.

Two uniform police officers had stopped by the school to speak with her. They were taking valuable time away from her planning period with their questions. The story was straightforward.

Gus had been an ass, and Ash had handled it.

End of story.

"What Officer Luther was saying was if there ever is a future time, to make sure you stay around and speak with the police before leaving," Officer Bunts said.

He smiled at her, but she wasn't in the mood to

smile. His gaze flickered over her, and her skin crawled.

"Yeah, well. I was scared and afraid and just left," she muttered, guiding them to her door. She had much more important things to do than sit around talking about a situation she just wanted to put behind her.

"Thank you for your time, ma'am. If we need anything, we'll be sure to be in touch," Officer Luther said.

She gave a nod and watched them walk down the hall of the school.

Her eyes connected with Erin's as she rushed from her room over to Deana.

"What was that all about?" she asked, following Deana into the room.

"The fight at the bar. They just had some questions about that night." Deana waved it off and sat in her chair behind her desk.

"I do, too." Erin chuckled. She crossed her arms in front of her chest. Her lips spread out into a wide grin. "So...what happened with you and Officer Fraser? I thought we were just going to forget about him."

"You did look at him, right?" Deana asked.

Memories of him stalking over to where she and Gus had been was ingrained into her mind. His dark shirt and jeans gave her plenty of ammunition for her dirty fantasies. His muscles had been well-defined, and his tattoos were on display.

How could she not leave with him? The only problem was, she had thought it was going to lead to something else.

Not being kissed to within an inch of her life and then pushed into the house to spend the night alone.

If I come inside tonight, I won't be leaving until tomorrow morning.

Just the replay of his words had her clamping her legs together.

She should have pulled his ass into her home and begged him to stay.

But she hadn't.

She'd been frozen in shock that he could just pull back from her and casually jog down her stairs and leave.

"So, what happened?" Erin lugged one of the chairs from her reading table over to Deana's desk. She sat and turned her attention to Deana.

"Nothing," she replied quietly.

"What do you mean 'nothing'? He literally fought a man for you, and you mean to tell me when you got back to your place nothing happened?" Erin's voice ended on a squeak. Her wide eyes met Deana's.

Deana shook her head slowly. She was at a loss, too.

"I really don't know. The kiss was—"

"Who kissed who?" Erin leaned in as if Deana had

the most juiciest gossip.

"He kissed me. It was amazing. I mean, stars and all. But before I knew it, he was putting me in the house and telling me to lock the door." Deana threw her hands up in the air. She sat back in her chair and crossed her legs.

It would appear she wasn't going to be able to get any work done before her class returned from gym.

"Weird." Erin tapped her finger on her chin, lost in her thoughts. "Did he call you at least?"

"I don't know how he would. We haven't exchanged phone numbers." Deana shrugged.

She had been pondering this situation all weekend. Ashton Fraser had left her completely frustrated and utterly confused.

A knock at the door drew their attention. A man in the postal service uniform stood at the door. Deana gasped, staring at what he had in his hand.

"I'm looking for Deana Dawson," he asked.

Deana stood in shock. Erin giggled and moved with her.

"I'm Deana Dawson," she murmured.

He pulled a clipboard from under his arm and thrust it toward her. His tired, weathered face showed that he couldn't care less about anything but having her sign. She scribbled her name on the paper and handed it back to him.

"Here you go." He passed her the large arrangement of flowers and turned on his heel and disappeared down the hallway.

"Those are beautiful," Erin gushed.

Deana held the bouquet of red roses and immediately put them up to her nose. She took in a deep breath and inhaled the aroma of the fresh-cut blooms.

"They smell good, too." She groaned.

Erin leaned in and took a whiff.

"Yes," she moaned, her eyes rolling into the back of her head. She focused on the card and pointed to it. "See who they are from."

They walked over to her desk. She set down the vase and plucked the card from the holder. Tearing open the envelope, she pulled the card free.

Beautiful flowers for a beautiful woman.
Be prepared for tomorrow.
I'm still going to kick your ass.
-Ash

Deana fell into a fit of giggles. She handed the card to Erin who joined her.

He hadn't forgotten their challenge.

She leaned down, getting another breath of the roses. Still no phone number. Looked like she'd just have to wait until the next day to see Ash.

Only she'd be doing the ass-kicking.

6

"I haven't played kickball since I was a kid." Myles chuckled, walking alongside Ash.

Ash had brought his friend along for moral support. There was no way he was going to battle and not have a second.

"It's a big deal here," Ash said.

The sun was shining bright, and the kids should be released for recess in a few minutes.

Ash was ready for today. He'd been imagining what Deana would wear for their competition. Not that she'd be wearing anything inappropriate, but to see her casual and letting loose was a fantasy of his.

It wasn't exactly how he wanted to see her let loose, but it would be a start.

"I hear. I haven't run around a diamond in about ten years." Myles gazed out onto the field. They made their way over to the fence that ran along the baseball field and leaned against it. "I'm old. These kids are probably going to run right over me."

"No matter how good of a shape you think you are, they will run all over you," Ash teased. "And they won't think twice about it. They are almost inhuman with all the energy they have."

He flexed his hand and found it to be still a little sore. It had scabbed over and was purplish from the bruising. So far it hadn't stopped him from working. Luckily enough, they hadn't had to go out on a SWAT call in the past few days.

The bell sounded off in the distance. It would only be a matter of time before the first kids exited the building to get to the playground. Ash turned just in time to see the doors of the school open.

A sea of children rushed out into single-file lines. Wide grins were present on every single kid as they made their way to the field. They picked up their speed, and within seconds they were fully fledged sprinting toward him.

"Officer Fraser!" Screams echoed through the air.

"Lucas. Chip." Ash stepped forward and held his hands up for the boys. They each slapped and gave him a high five. "Ready for some kickball?"

"Heck yeah! Miss Dawson went to change her clothes. Her and Miss Fletcher have been talking trash all day," Lucas said.

"They have?" He chuckled, glancing over at Myles. "Fellas, let me introduce you to my partner, Officer Burton."

"What's up, guys," Myles greeted them with an outstretched hand.

The boys' chests puffed out slightly as they each shook Myles's hand.

Both boys were being raised by a single mother. They were good kids, and it helped them to have some example of respectable men in their lives. Even if it was only once or twice a week. Ash and the other cops involved tried to instill some life lessons while working with the kids.

"We've been waiting for this day since last week!" Chip exclaimed.

"Yeah? Why?" Myles asked them.

"Officer Fraser challenged Miss Dawson to the kickball challenge. She never participates in the games." Lucas shook his head.

"She's always dressed up and in high heels." Chip giggled.

"Yeah, Chip always talks about how pretty she is," Lucas teased.

"I do not!" Chip shouted, stepping closer to Lucas. His eyes narrowed on Lucas, and his hands balled into tight fists.

Ash stepped forward and separated the boys. He

ignored Myles's chuckle.

He didn't blame Chip one bit for always looking at Deana. She certainly had his attention.

"Hey, guys. That's enough. Let's get ready for the game," he said, trying to hide his chuckle. "Now go get the ball and get the teams ready."

The boys scampered off, shouting for their classmates.

"Looks likes you certainly know how to negotiate with the kids," Myles remarked.

Ash glanced at him and rolled his eyes. It was no different than when they were in a hostage situation. He had to understand the targets and get them to trust him.

He turned back. His attention landed on the object of his desires, and he froze.

Deana. Fucking. Dawson.

In shorts, a tank top, and tennis shoes.

His gaze greedily roamed her body as she moved closer to him. Her warm-brown legs were on display, and his heart raced. His perusal made its way up to her face, and he was met by the most determined stare.

She smirked as she arrived in front of him.

"Officer Fraser," she said.

Miss Fletcher was at her side with a wide grin.

"Miss Dawson." His voice came out strangled. He

coughed to clear his throat and nodded to Miss Fletcher. "Did you receive my reminder?"

It had been a last-minute decision to send her flowers. He felt Myles's eyes on him. He didn't want to say what he'd sent. Myles would have his balls if he knew he was out sending women flowers.

"Yes, I did. Thank you. I just hope you brought your A game with you today." She smirked.

Ash wanted to lean forward and capture her lips with his. Memories of their kiss floated around in his head, and he could have kicked himself for leaving that night.

Now was not the time for kissing Deana.

It was kickball time.

"Oh, I brought it and my partner. Myles Burton, this is Deana Dawson and Erin Fletcher." He quickly reintroduced them. He took note of the way Erin's eyes lit up when they landed on Myles.

"Nice to meet you under better circumstances," Myles said.

"I thought you looked familiar. You were out with Officer Fraser the other night." Deana nodded while shaking Myles's hand.

"Yes, ma'am. Someone has to keep this one out of trouble." He chuckled, pointing to Ash.

"You didn't too well of a job. If I remember, you

were right there next to me," Ash said, turning to Myles.

"So you needed backup today?" Her perfectly arched eyebrow rose. "Couldn't handle little ol' me?"

He instantly got her underlining meaning. He could handle her all right. She just didn't know who she'd just challenged.

He was Ashton Fraser.

His lips spread into a grin, and a chuckle escaped him. "Oh, I can handle you." He turned to Myles who was grinning from ear to ear. "I'll give you Myles and I'll play on Miss Fletcher's team."

"Bring it on, Officer Fraser." She spread her hands out while the kids laughed. They pulled her onto the field while instantly gathering with their respected classes.

"Let's play some kickball!" he called out.

The kids cheered. He jogged out to the field with the rest of Miss Fletcher's class.

"Since this has been all the talk of school, I'll officiate the coin toss!" Mr. Sims, the sixth-grade teacher said, jogging out onto the field. He waved Deana and Ash over. They both arrived at the pitching mound at the same time. They playfully scowled at each other. "I'm neutral, and the kids have been talking about this nonstop. So since this is a big game, there needs to be an official coin toss."

"Fair enough," Deana said, laughing.

Deana's eyes sparkled, and Ash's lips turned up in the corner. Her warm and bubbly personality was infectious. This was how he always wanted to see her. The usual shy demeanor was gone, and this was the carefree Deana.

"Okay. Here's the quarter. Two different sides," Mr. Sims joked. He held it up for both of them to see. They both nodded, approving the coin. "Who is calling it?"

"I'll let the lady call it," Ash said, motioning to Deana.

"How kind of you, sir." Deana batted her lashes and poured on her southern accent.

"Okay. Here we go." Mr. Sims tossed the coin in the air and caught it with his hand. He placed it on the back of his other hand and kept it covered. He turned to Deana and waited for her to bet.

She stared at Ash, her plump lips curled up in a smile. "Heads."

Mr. Sims removed his hand, and Ash's gaze flickered to the coin.

"Heads, it is! Miss Dawson's team is kicking first!" Mr. Sims called out.

Deana stuck out her tongue and spun away, jogging back over to her team.

Ash barked a laugh at her silliness.

He returned to his team. The little schoolteacher was lucky they were around so many kids and the other teachers.

He had about a million things cross his mind on what she could be doing with her cute little tongue.

"Way to go, Chad!" Deana shouted. Her student had kicked the ball far enough where he landed on second base. She glanced around and rolled her eyes.

Shit.

It was her turn to kick.

Her heart pounded while she walked up to the home plate. Her name was being shouted by the kids, and she felt all eyes on her. It would seem the entire school was watching their game. Kids of all grades were gathered around the fence, cheering their favorite classroom on.

She gazed out to the pitcher's mound. Ash stood there with a devilish grin. She swallowed hard, trying to ignore the way his t-shirt showed off his muscular form. Memories of being crushed up against him encouraged a shiver to slide down her spine.

"You can do it, Miss Dawson!" one of her kids shouted.

"Do I need to take it easy on you? Let you warm up a bit?" Ash called out.

Had her kids not been around, she may have flipped him off.

"Roll the ball, Officer Fraser," she hollered.

Deana bounced on the balls of her feet to show she was ready; she was in shape. She maybe a little curvy, but she did work out—she ran a few times a week and did her yoga.

Deana could kick a ball and run around the bases.

No problem.

Ignoring the shrieking and screaming, she focused on the ball rolling her way, and ran forward and kicked with all her might, sending the ball skyrocketing through the air.

Deana screamed and took off running. Cheers echoed while she rounded first base. She continued to run and saw Chad sliding home. A few kids in Erin's class were running back with the ball. She made it to second base and stopped. The kid on second laughed at how out of breath she was.

"Oh my," she gasped, fighting to drag air into her burning lungs.

It had not been as easy as she thought. What in the world had she been thinking? Her lungs screamed as she tried to gulp in air. She leaned over and rested her hands on her knees.

"You okay, Miss Dawson?" he asked.

She nodded and was finally able to catch her breath. The kid's name escaped her at the moment. "Yes, I'm okay."

"Let me know if you need to sit out the game," Ash called out.

She narrowed her eyes on him and shook her head. "I'm just fine. Roll the ball."

He threw her a wink and turned back to the next player. A young girl from her class named Raina was up to kick.

"Let's go, Raina!" Deana encouraged, edging away from the base.

Raina gave her a thumbs-up and scrunched her face in concentration.

Ash glanced over his shoulder at her, and she paused. She could easily jump back to the base if he tried to get her out.

She stuck her tongue out at him, and his gaze narrowed on her.

Maybe I shouldn't have done that, she thought. That stare of his made her want to rip her clothes off.

Down girl.

There are kids around.

He turned back around, and she took another step away from the base, ready to run the minute Raina kicked the ball.

Ash rolled the ball to Raina who ran forward and kicked it. The ball soared through the air and landed somewhere between second base and the pitcher's mound.

Deana took off running. She pumped her arms hard, heading for third base.

"Throw it!" Ash yelled out.

She was halfway to third and saw Ash with the ball in his hand. He rushed toward her, gaining on her fast. She squealed and felt him reach her. The ball slammed into her hip just as she hopped onto the base. She lost her balance and tumbled over onto the ground.

She rolled to a stop and broke out into an uncontrollable fit of laughter. Ash arrived over to her with a wide grin on his lips.

"Safe!" she yelled, breathless. She sat up, breathing hard, and looked around.

The kids were in an uproar, screaming and laughing. Excitement was in the air from the game.

"I don't know about that. I got you out!" He shook his head and offered her his hand.

"I demand an umpire!" She laughed. Taking his hand, she stood. She released a cry and fell into him as her knee gave out.

"I got you. Are you all right?" Concern lined Ash's face, and he glanced down at her. He wrapped an arm around her waist.

It was then she took notice of the pain in her knee. It throbbed, and she tried to take a step on it, but a cry tore from her lips. She leaned on Ash's muscular form. She had thought of pushing herself against him again, but this was not how she had imagined it.

"Goodness, that hurts." She bit her lip.

"Up you go," Ash said. He hoisted her up in his arms and began carrying her away from the field.

The kids stood around with worry on their faces.

"Take her to the nurse's office," Erin said, jogging up to them. Her gaze met Deana's before shifting to Deana's leg. "Your knee is already swelling. Looks like we'll have to take a rain check on the rest of the game."

"I'm fine—"

"I'm taking you to the nurse. That's it," Ash cut her off and walked toward the school.

She closed her mouth at his stern look.

"Thanks, Ash. I'll handle the kids!" Erin called out.

"Thanks, Miss Fletcher!" she responded. The stubborn set of Ash's jaw let her know she would not be winning this argument.

7

"Ash, I can walk! That's what the crutches are for!" Deana exclaimed. She waved around the crutches.

"Hold on before I drop you," he threatened. Her arm tightened around his neck. He wouldn't drop her but he certainly would threaten to do so.

He jogged up the stairs to her home and paused at the door. It was his fault that she was in the predicament she was in. Had he just let her get to the base, she wouldn't have fallen and sprained her knee.

When the nurse had taken one look at Deana's knee, she'd recommended they take her to the emergency room to be assessed since it had swelled so quickly.

"Keys," he demanded.

"I can do it. Your hands are currently full." She smirked. She reached in her purse and pulled out her keys.

"I'm good at multitasking," he bragged.

She snorted and ignored his outstretched fingers. She inserted the key into the lock and turned it. The door opened, and Ash pushed it forward more. He stepped in and kicked it shut with his foot.

"Ash, put me down. I'll hop over to the couch." She giggled.

He loved the sound of her laughter and shook his head. His gaze swept her small home, and he saw touches of her throughout.

Her front door faced the stairway that led to the second floor. The living room was to his right with the dining room to the left.

It was cozy but modern and instantly gave Ash the feeling that Deana had made this a true home. His heart skipped a beat at the thought of settling down and creating such a haven.

He froze for a second.

What was so bad about settling down? Look at Mac and Declan. They had been against taking a wife. Everyone knew that. Now, they were both locked down with a ball and chain.

Ash loved Sarena and Aspen as if they were sisters. They completed both Mac and Declan.

He glanced down at Deana's sparkling eyes, and a grin spread.

There wasn't anything wrong at all. Hell, if he'd learned anything from Mac and Dec, it was to find a good woman and then do anything in your power to keep her.

Even go to war.

Both of his brothers in blue had almost lost their women. Thankfully, their team had banded together as they always did and ensured the girls were safe.

His feet automatically carried them to the couch. Sitting her gently on it, he knelt before her.

"What's up with the silly grin?" she asked. She tilted her head to the side, studying him.

"Nothing. Was just thinking how cute you are," he responded. He reached for her tennis shoes and slid them off her feet.

"Mmm-hmm..." She tapped her chin with her finger, the sparkle still there in her eyes. "I'm thinking you are buttering me up for something."

"What? Who, me?" He feigned surprise and hurt.

She swatted at him, and he dodged her hand while standing. He fell onto the couch and brought her legs up to lay them across his lap.

"Thank you, Ash," she murmured, her smile slowly disappearing.

He languidly rubbed her foot, and a sigh released from her lips.

"It's all my fault." He shrugged and met her stare.

"I'm just clumsy. I didn't even realize I had hurt myself until I stood up."

He encircled her small foot with his large hands. Everything about her was petite, and he loved it. He was much taller than her, and she just brought out his protective side. He ached to slide his hands up higher on her smooth brown calves.

They'd spent a couple hours at the emergency room before they'd discharged her home to his care.

Tonight, he would stay with her to ensure she could get around.

"So what's your favorite type of food?" he asked, thinking of the few restaurants he could order from to be delivered.

"You don't have to order out. I can cook something." She tried to pull her foot away, but he held on tight and shook his head.

"Doctor said for you to stay off the leg for a day or two. I'll take care of dinner tonight." He ran a finger down her foot, and she squealed. He laughed at her reaction.

Little did she know, she already had him wrapped around her little finger. He didn't even care. Everything about her was genuine, and he appreciated it. There had been plenty of women—police groupies—wanting a piece of him because he was a man in uniform, and with his SWAT decal, it was like he and his team were superstars.

"So will this be our first date?" Her perfectly sculpted eyebrow rose high.

"Nope." He shook his head. "A date with Ashton Fraser is a big deal. Let's consider this a pregame."

She rolled her eyes at his teasing. Her lips curved up into a smile. Ash was learning that he loved to make her laugh and smile.

No, this wouldn't be their first date. That day would be coming as soon as she was cleared to walk. He wanted to make sure it would be a night she could get dressed up and wear her heels for him.

His cock stiffened with the thought of her legs in her infamous heels.

Down boy, he muttered to himself.

"Well, in that case, I hear that Romano's is delivering now," she suggested.

Ash grabbed his phone from his pocket with a wide grin. He was careful to hold her legs on his lap. "Whatever the lady wants, the lady gets."

"I could get used to this." She leaned back on the couch and stretched. Her t-shirt rode up, revealing her navel.

Sweat broke out on his forehead.

He swore and looked away, unable to believe how his body was reacting to her. It was as if he was fifteen again, trying to make it to third base with a girl.

"You know the number?" he asked.

"I have one of their menus in the drawer next to the fridge," she said.

He carefully removed her legs and stood from the couch. Grabbing one of the throw pillows, he positioned it underneath her injured knee. "Don't move. I'll be right back."

"Not going anywhere." She giggled.

He tossed her a wink and made his way toward the kitchen.

Deana's cheeks hurt from laughing so much. Ash was animated in telling her stories of the craziest missions he'd been on. The current one about a naked bad guy had tears sliding down her cheeks.

"So you had to handcuff him naked?" she asked, placing her plate down on the coffee table. She was officially stuffed. Ash had ordered enough food to feed a small army. She glanced over to his plate and wasn't sure where he packed all of it.

His body was toned and muscular. She was sure there wasn't an ounce of fat on him. Totally the opposite of her. She was sure the lasagna had gone straight to her hips. She'd have to up her workouts as soon as her knee was better.

"I swear the guy had lathered himself in oil or

something. When we finally got our hands on him, he was on the ground with three of us on top of him. Iker and Myles had to hold him down while I put the handcuffs on his wrists." He took sip of his drink while Deana fell into a fit of laughter. Ash shook his head and rolled his eyes.

"But why was he naked?" she asked.

"Hell if I know. He was probably high on something." Ash shrugged, setting his glass down. "All I know is once he was loaded up in the squad car, he was no longer my concern." He stretched his arms out on the back of the couch.

Deana bit her lip and saw an open opportunity. The entire night, her body had been strung tight, and she refused to let the evening end with him leaving her alone and frustrated.

Not again.

Damn her busted knee.

She slid across the couch and positioned herself into him. He glanced down with a surprised look. A grin spread across his lips as he wrapped his arm around her shoulder, pulling her close, leaving no room between them.

Deana's heart raced at the feel of his muscular build pressed against her. She'd never been one to make the first move before, so this was unchartered territory.

"This was fun," she said. She cringed internally at the huskiness of her voice.

"Yeah, it was," he agreed. His hand tightened on her arm while the other one came over and tipped her chin up higher.

She held her breath as he leaned down and covered her lips in the sweetest kiss she'd ever experienced.

A groan escaped her. Ash took advantage of her mouth opening and pushed his tongue forth to meet hers.

Deana celebrated inside. Somehow Ash lifted her from the couch and settled her onto his lap. Her legs rested on the couch to give her knee room to stretch out.

She wrapped her arms around his neck and angled her head to the side. She was becoming lost in the kiss, never wanting it to end. Ash crushed her chest to his. The hardness pressing against her hip had her whimpering.

He reached up and gripped the back of her neck with one hand holding her in place as he plundered her mouth. Her breasts grew heavy with a tingling sensation running through them. She needed to feel his touch on them.

As if knowing what she was thinking, his other hand cupped her one breast. Needing his hands on her bare flesh, Deana reached down and gripped the edge of her shirt and pulled it over her head, breaking their kiss. She tossed her top over her shoulder while watching Ash's gaze drop to her lace-covered mounds. She was desperate to straddle him, but her bum knee wouldn't allow her to bend it all the way, so it looked as if she was stuck sitting sidesaddle on his lap.

"Are you sure?" Ash asked, his heated gaze meeting hers.

Her breaths were coming fast in anticipation of what was to come. She bit her lip and nodded, unable to verbally respond. If she did, she sure wouldn't be a lady.

He leaned forward and reached behind her with one hand, bringing their faces close. She leaned forward and nipped his bottom lip, eliciting a growl from him. Their gazes locked together, and he gently freed her from the lace contraption. The straps loosened on her shoulders and slid down to rest on her arms.

His hands brushed the cups aside while he pulled it off. His gaze was on her breasts, and her heart stuttered. Her nipples hardened to tight buds, the cold air brushing them.

Deana glanced down and watched him cup her now freed breast. He gripped it tight before rolling her nipple between his fingers, and she groaned. He sat up on the couch, keeping her on his lap. His breath slowly blew against her neck while he continued to massage her mound.

"Ash," she moaned.

He gently nipped her shoulder and brought her against his chest. She angled her head away from him, offering her neck to him. His chest vibrated with a chuckle. He slowly ran his tongue along the curve of her neck.

Her core clenched with need.

"Deana, do you know how much I want you?"

She whimpered and shook her head. The hard evidence of his desire pressed against her was all she needed to get a quick clue. His hand released her breast and slid down the soft swell of her tummy. It landed on her button of her shorts and freed it.

"So fucking bad," he muttered.

He leaned her back along the arm of the sofa while he worked her shorts open. He eased them and her panties down her legs. Using her good leg, she kicked them both off, leaving her naked on his lap.

Deana watched him take her in, and any insecurity she may have had about her body completely disappeared. His eyes darkened, and his tongue snuck out and licked his lips as if he was about to devour her.

Just that thought had moisture seeping out of her core. She was slick with need. He ran a hand along her thigh, sending chills through her.

Deana parted her legs to allow his hand to slide between them.

"Ash," she whispered. She reached up and gripped his shirt as he parted her slick folds. Her body arched off his lap when his finger found her clitoris.

"Just hold on, baby. I got you." A cocky grin appeared on his lips.

His gaze flickered to hers, and she knew she was about to be in for the ride of her life.

He dipped his finger inside her, drawing a deep moan from her. His other hand gripped her breast and gently massaged it while his finger trailed along the length of her folds before making its way back to her swollen nub.

I guess he didn't lie about being a multitasker, she thought to herself with a laugh.

Ash strummed her clit, and her breath caught in her throat. Her eyes drew shut, and she basked in the feeling of him working her toward an orgasm.

It had been a while since she'd had one that she hadn't brought on herself.

Deana didn't even want to think about the sight she must have made. She felt every bit of a wanton hussy lying on Ash's lap naked with his hand buried between her legs.

Deana gasped from the slight pain of him pinching her nipple. She writhed on his lap while he flicked her clit faster. Her heart raced, making it harder for her to breathe. Her chest was rising and falling fast with her trying to drag in air.

Deana cried out, rocking her hips against his hand. He slipped one finger deep into drenched channel then added a second one. She opened her legs wider to accommodate him. He pushed his fingers farther before pulling them out. He thrust them back in, hard and fast.

"Oh God! Ash," she whimpered, loving the feeling, but she wanted more.

Her pussy clenched around his fingers. But what she really needed was Ash's thick length to slide deep inside her.

She balled his shirt into her fist, needing to hold on to something. Her cries filled the air while her body trembled.

"Come on, Deana. Let it go." His voice was deep and sexy. He left his fingers buried and rubbed her nub with his thumb.

The pressure of him pressing down on her clit sent her skyrocketing to the heavens.

She threw her head back against the sofa arm and cried out. She moaned her way through the sensations coursing through her body.

"Oh my," she sighed, unsure what to say, floating

back to reality. She covered her face with her hands, somewhat embarrassed.

"Why are you covering your face?" Ash chuckled.

He removed her hand, and her eyes flickered open and met his. They stared at each other for what seemed like hours, but it was only a minute or so.

"That was fucking beautiful."

He withdrew his fingers from her and brought them to his lips. Lust for him slammed into her chest as she watched him lick his fingers clean.

"Ash." Her voice was strangled when he turned his focus back to her. She sat up on his lap with his help and reached for him. He slammed his lips down on hers in a hard kiss. Her mouth automatically opened to grant his tongue entry.

The sound of a phone ringing off in the distance had both of them freezing in place.

Ash released a curse. "You have got to be fucking kidding me." He pulled back away from her and glanced over at his phone. "I'm sorry. I have to take that."

She shifted off of him to allow him to grab his phone. Goosebumps slid along her skin. She reached for the throw blanket she kept on the back of her sofa and covered herself.

"Fraser," he snapped, answering the call.

He flopped back down on the couch and turned his

gaze to her. He glared at the blanket and tugged at it as if it offended him. She held tight with a giggle. Her laughter faded as he paused to listen to the other person on the phone.

A seriousness settled on his face while he continued to listen to whoever was on the other line. "I'll be right there."

He disconnected the call and released a deep sigh.

"You have to go?" she asked, already knowing the answer. A call this late to a SWAT officer only meant one thing.

He nodded and stood from the couch. He leaned down over her, pressing his hands into the back of the couch. He touched his lips to hers, hard, in bruising kiss.

"This isn't over," he murmured, pulling back slightly.

She blinked to focus and met his gaze. The glint in his eyes had a shiver passing through her body.

He ran a hand along her cheek. "Not by a long shot, Deana."

"Be careful." She didn't even want to think of the danger he put himself in.

"Always."

8

Ash released a curse. His fucking balls were probably dark blue and hanging on by a thread. He gripped his MP5 tight to fight checking on his cock and balls. He had flown out of Deana's home and down to the station.

For the first time since making SWAT he'd had thoughts of not responding to a call. It couldn't have come at a worse moment. A few minutes more and he would have been sliding deep inside Deana.

He leaned his helmet-covered head back against the wall of the BEAR.

The memory of her naked body writhing on his lap had his dick pressing against his pants. Her curvy brown form called to him and left him wanting to take his time discovering every inch of it. Her body had been so responsive to him.

The taste of her still lingered on his tongue.

This isn't over, Deana.

His words echoed in his mind, and he would keep the promise. There was no way after just one taste of her would he be able to stay away from her.

"Daydreaming over there, Fraser?" Mac's voice cut into his thoughts.

He turned and met the gaze of his sergeant.

"No, sir," he replied. He felt all eyes on him. He leaned forward, trying to adjust his damn cock which had a mind of its own. He sent up a prayer it would go down. There would be no way he could enter a potential gunfight with a hard-on.

"Wouldn't do us any good if you were sleeping on the job," Mac snapped. He turned his attention to the rest of the team. "Tonight, we have a drugged-out male in a third-story apartment we need to apprehend. He has weapons, and shots have been fired from his apartment window. Hence why we are being called in."

Ash shook off the images of Deana and concentrated on Mac. His sergeant was right. He could put the entire team in danger if he wasn't completely focused on the mission at hand.

"According to the intel, Marshall Good has been wanted on drug trafficking and evading police. Police were called at twenty-one hundred hours to the address thought to be his," Declan announced, taking over. "We are to capture him and bring him to justice."

Nods went around the BEAR. The mission sounded easy, but it could go to hell in the blink of an eye.

Ash was confident that his team would do well. They practiced this exact procedure hundreds of times to ensure their entry into such a dangerous situation would be flawless and without casualty.

Tonight, they had a real deranged character with plenty of guns at his disposal.

"Have there been any attempt at negotiations?" Ash asked. It was his specialty. He'd talked many drugged-out bad guys out of similar situations before.

"We bypassed that when he started shooting at our boys in blue," Mac replied dryly.

Ash nodded and tightened his grip on his weapon. The BEAR slowed to a halt.

"Let's get this motherfucker," Myles growled next to Ash.

"SWAT," Mac barked. The air in the vehicle grew tense. "Let's hunt."

Brody swung open the door and jumped down from the vehicle. Ash pulled his face mask on and followed with the others exiting behind him. They gathered on the side of the BEAR, hidden from the view of the assailant.

He took in the street. Black-and-white cars lined the area. There were civilians being pushed back away from the building. A few news channel vans were parked on the corner of the street, and he was sure they were trying to catch every detail for their stories.

Mac immediately began yelling orders to the beat cops, taking control of the situation in true Mac fashion. The rest of the team gathered around Declan who would issue their direction.

"How are we entering?" Iker asked.

"Has the rest of the building been evacuated?" Zain questioned.

Ash stepped back and glanced around the vehicle to look at the building. It was a three-story that appeared to house two apartments on each floor. The front had a fire escape on the outside that could provide a way of entry.

"Yes. All civilians residing in the building have been moved to safety. We're to secure the apartment and subdue the target," Declan began. "Team B is Brodie, Iker, and Zain who will be going through the apartment door."

"Yes, sir," Brodie murmured.

Iker and Zain shifted to stand next to him while they continued listening to the plan. Brodie moved to the side of the BEAR and opened the compartment that held his mini ram.

"Team A will be me and Ash who will be going up

the fire escape. We'll throw a few flash-bangs in through the windows. Once the bang goes off, I want that door breached by Team B and the apartment secured. Myles, you need to be posted over there, covering our asses as we go up the fire escape. If that fucker tries to shoot, you have orders to fire."

"Kill shot?" Myles's eyebrow tilted up. He was an excellent sniper and could hit a mark in any place he chose. His time as a ranger had helped him hone his skills as a deadly sniper. It was a much-needed skill to have while serving on a SWAT team.

"Hell no. You want the mayor's office on our asses?" Declan snorted.

Ash shoved Myles with his elbow. He could see his friend's eyes crinkle in the corner and knew he was grinning behind his face mask.

"Incapacitate him."

"Got it." Myles nodded before turning to leave. He jogged away to find an area he would be able to have a clear shot at the target.

"Are we sure he's alone in there?" Iker asked, moving to look at the building.

"From what we know, he is. But we're not going to take any chances. Mac will be working with the sergeant who was in charge to make sure the perimeter is secured. This should be a standard mission. He'll be our backup if we need anything," Declan said. He met the eyes of each team member. "Any questions?"

Ash shook his head. They were briefed with what they needed to know. Shouting of incomprehensible words could be heard from the apartment's open window. They target was escalating. There was no telling what he was high on, and that made this extremely dangerous.

Drugs and weapons didn't go well together, and from the looks of it, he had access to both.

"No."

Voices echoed around them.

"Let's sync up our communicators now," Declan ordered.

Ash reached up and hit the tiny device that was already in his ear. When they needed to communicate with each other, the little earbuds allowed them to hear each other within a few miles' radius.

"Testing," Zain murmured, his voice coming through clear in Ash's ear.

"Confirmed," Iker responded first.

Each man replied the same to ensure they were all set up.

"Be careful out there. Holler if you need me," Mac's voice came over the connection.

Ash moved over to the BEAR and opened one of the compartments on the side. He secured his MP5 in another compartment. For this mission, he'd have to use his Glock. Since he and Declan would be in charge of subduing the target, he would need to grab a few of the grenades.

He reached in and pulled two M84 stun grenades from the storage compartment. The small device was a non-lethal way to subdue an individual or bring order to a crowd. He secured the grenades in his cargo pants and shut the door.

"If there are no other questions, then let's move. Heads up and stay sharp," Declan ordered.

They would approach the building in standard formation before splitting up.

Ash hoisted his weapon up in his hands and focused. They lined up with Brody in the front.

They quickly made their way around the BEAR and headed toward the building.

Ash's breaths slowed. He kept his weapon trained on the building and swept the property. His body grew tense while he drew closer. They had to be careful to ensure the target didn't come out shooting as they approached.

They moved in sync with each other, having done this a countless amount of times. They arrived on the sidewalk that led up to the building. The front door was in sight.

Ash felt Declan close behind him. He motioned for

Declan to follow him. No words would be needed. Their hand signals would be all that was necessary.

He'd go up the fire escape first with Declan immediately behind him. The rest of the team disappeared through the front door while Ash and Declan made their way to the stairs. They arrived at the building and put their back against it to make themselves less of a target should the shooter lean out of the window.

Ash glanced at Dec who gave him a nod. He jumped slightly up in the air and grabbed the last bar of the stairs. Ash quickly pulled himself up.

Thanks to their intense training and workouts, it was a breeze with all his gear on. He quietly climbed the stairs and drew the first grenade out his pocket then paused to wait for Declan.

The metal stairs jerked as Declan followed. He stalked up a few stairs while brandishing his weapon back. He would be Ash's cover since he didn't have his gun in his hand.

Their eyes met, and Dec gave a slight nod. It was time to move closer to the open window.

Cursing and threats filtered out while they slowly walked up the stairs.

"Fuck!" a hoarse voice screamed.

Ash slowed his steps, eyeing the window.

"Leave me the hell alone!"

Ash and Declan pressed close to the building. The voice came from the opening of the window. Ash sent a small prayer up that Marshall wouldn't look down and see two men crawling up the fire escape.

"Team A, you're good. He's not leaning out the window," Mac's soft voice came through the ear bud.

Ash breathed a sigh of relief. They continued up until they reached the landing below his window. It was off to the side, and a few steps would put them directly in front of the target's window.

They paused and leaned back against the railing.

"Team B, report," Mac's voice came through again.

"We're in position," Brodie replied. "The door isn't heavy-duty. Should give way with one if not two hits."

"Team A, now," Mac ordered.

Ash pushed off the wall and slowly crawled up the few stairs, bringing him closer to the open window. He snatched the pin out of the grenade and tossed it in. One second later, a loud bang echoed through the air along with a bright flash of light.

Declan flew up the stairs behind him with his gun trained on the window. Ash drew his weapon out of his thigh holster and followed behind him.

"Police department!" someone shouted from the inside.

Yelling broke out as they entered through the

window. Brodie and the others were entering through the door. Ash kept his weapon trained in the air.

The target was on the floor, stunned from the impact of the grenade. Zain flipped him over and secured his wrists behind him with zip ties.

"Clear the entire apartment," Declan ordered.

"Is anyone else in here with you?" Zain yelled at the suspect.

Brodie stood next to him with his gun trained on him.

Ash followed behind Declan as they moved away from the living room. His breaths were coming fast. Declan kicked a closed door open, and they both ducked by the walls first. Ash was first to peek through, finding no one in the office. He pushed off the wall and kept his gun aimed true. He quickly stalked in with Declan right behind him. He swept the room with his gun to ensure no one was hiding in any corner.

They focused on the single door and moved toward it. Declan slipped next to it while Ash kept his gun pointed at it. His muscles tensed in anticipation. Their intel said the guy was the only one in the apartment, but they had to sweep it to be sure.

He gave a nod.

Declan swung the it open.

"Clear," Ash called out.

There was nothing in the small closet except a few

wire hangers swinging from the pole and a couple of pairs of shoes on the floor.

"Clear," Iker checked in.

"Clear," Zain was next.

Ash breathed a sigh of relief. It was as they said it would be. A quick breach and capture.

Just what he needed. No casualties or persons shot that would require extensive paperwork.

A quick in and out.

"Mac, the apartment is secured," Declan announced, walking out the room.

Ash followed behind him. In just a short few minutes, they had breached and invaded the property and had it secured.

"Good job, men," Mac announced through the communicators.

Zain and Brodie pulled the handcuffed prisoner up off the floor and practically dragged him out. His muttered curses could be heard from the hallway.

"Perfect execution tonight, men," Declan praised them. He waved them toward the exit.

They filed out of the apartment to allow it to get processed.

"Thank goodness that was quick," Zain muttered. "I have a date with my pillow, and she is calling my name."

Ash snorted. It was late, and there was no way he'd

make it back to Deana's at a decent time. He might as well chalk it up and head home.

Looked like he'd have to be his own date tonight to relieve the blueness from his balls.

9

"So he hasn't called you at all?" Erin scoffed. She followed Deana into her home.

"No. I imagine he's been busy." Deana sighed. That could be the only reason she could think of where Ash wouldn't at least call her.

It had been three days since the night she'd fallen apart in Ash's arms. He'd left out on a call and hadn't been heard of since.

She limped toward the kitchen, unable to sit on her couch with her friend. Her cheeks heated with the thought of her writhing naked while lying across Ash's lap.

"Your kids have been missing you something fierce," Erin stated.

"I miss them, too." Deana dropped her keys and purse on the counter. She hobbled toward the fridge and pried it open. She stared at the contents, not finding anything appealing. "Want to order out?" she asked, looking over her shoulder.

"I do have a hankering for Chinese food." Erin rubbed her flat belly.

Deana rolled her eyes while beating down the little hint of jealousy. She wished she was a slim as Erin. Deana was just a curvy girl, and there was really nothing she could do. Even if she lost weight, her hips and butt weren't going anywhere.

"Look in that drawer near you and there should be a menu for Wong's." Deana pointed toward the cabinet while reaching in and grabbing a bottle of cheap wine she'd kept in the fridge.

"Sweet. What do you have a taste for? I'll call it in," Erin offered, reading the menu.

"Sesame chicken for me, please."

While Erin rang in their order, Deana slowly made her way to the cabinet where she stored her wine glasses. It had been a few days since the fall, and she'd just come from the doctor's. After examining it, the doctor thought she should be able to go back to work on Monday.

Ice and relaxation for her this weekend.

Deana poured them both healthy glasses of wine. Erin was still on her cell placing their order. Deana set a glass on the counter near her.

Deana's knee was slightly sore, but it felt much better than it had when she'd tried to stand up on the baseball field. She took a sip of the sweet wine, and her mind returned to Ash. Before he'd left her, he had programmed his number into her cell.

She'd been too chicken to call him. Grabbing her phone from her purse, she stared down at it as if willing it to ring.

"Why don't you call him?" Erin suggested, hanging up. She reached for her glass and took an unladylike gulp.

"Is it too much for me to want him to come after me?" she asked. She fiddled with her glass and leaned against the counter.

Deana couldn't help that she was a southern girl at heart and believed the man should be pursuing her.

"Girl, in this day and age, women go after men. There isn't anything wrong with making sure he knows the interest is there." Erin laughed.

"But—"

"And you said when he left it was for work." Erin wagged a finger at her. "My sister knows a couple cops, and she heard that the SWAT guys are badass and get called out for the most dangerous situations that regular cops aren't trained for."

"I know you are supposed to be making me feel

better, but now I'm worried about him." She blew out a deep breath and scooped up her cell from the counter.

"Then just call him," Erin urged.

Deana bit her lip and stared down at the screen again. She hadn't told Erin the entire story. If she had, her friend would be screaming for her to call him so he could come back to finish her off.

She couldn't remember the last time she'd had an orgasm as explosive as the one she'd had on Ash's finger.

Not his tongue.

Not his cock.

He'd made her come with his fingers, and she was craving more.

"Okay." She slid her thumb across the glass screen and scrolled to his name and hit it, placing the phone against her ear. Her heart raced as she waited for him to answer. Erin's lips spread into a wide grin. Deana turned her back to her friend. It rang a few times before his voicemail picked up. She hesitated but went ahead and left a message.

"Hey, Ash. It's me, Deanna. I was thinking about you and I—" She paused. What should she say? She missed him? She wanted to see him? She wanted him? She chuckled then sighed. "Just call me when you get a chance, okay. I hope everything is all right."

She disconnected the call and faced Erin, confused.

"Oh no, puppy-dog face." Erin rushed forward and took the phone from her and sat it on the table. "I'm sure he's busy. He'll call you. If not, you are bound to see him next week at the school."

"I'm not making a fool of myself, am I?" she asked. She took a sip of her wine, and they headed into the living room. Her gaze connected with the couch, and her core clenched.

Holy moly.

How was she ever going to get the memory of them on the sofa out of her mind?

She couldn't even look at it without thinking of Ash.

"No. You are not. I have an idea."

Deana glanced at Erin, and the smile that spread across her friend's face left her quite suspicious.

"I don't know about your plans." Deana giggled, shaking her head.

"Oh, come on!" Erin barked a laugh. She had to have seen the distrust on Deana's face. "I'm not that bad."

Deana took another sip of her wine and shook her head. Did she even want to know the plan her friend was cooking up?

Ash didn't know if he was coming or going. Every single day SWAT had been called out. He didn't know what was going on, but there had been an increase in calls lately.

Four days ago, he'd been almost about to go to Heaven with Deana in his arms.

Instead, he'd ended up in Hell.

He'd barely slept, having caught a couple hours here and there at the station. It had been pointless to go home.

He and his team had been out on raids apprehending dangerous criminals who had warrants, a hostage situation, and were even called in to assist the FBI.

His body was screaming for a good twenty-four of sleep. That wasn't too much to ask for.

Walking through the locker room, he nodded to a few officers. He opened his locker and grabbed his cell. He had a few missed calls, but one in particular stood out. He swiped the screen and hit his voicemails.

Deana had left him a message.

He tapped on it and lifted the phone up to his ear.

"Hey, Ash. It's me, Deanna. I was thinking about you and I—" She paused. *"Just call me when you get a chance, okay. I hope everything is all right."*

The message ended. He closed his eyes briefly before they snapped open. He looked at his watch and saw that school should be letting out soon. Glancing down at himself, he realized he was sweaty, dirty, and there are a few questionable stains on his pants and shirt.

He couldn't go to her dressed and smelling like this.

If he did nothing else, he needed a shower.

Twenty minutes later, he was back at his locker feeling rejuvenated. Excitement at seeing Deana filled his chest. It didn't matter that he hadn't slept, he needed to see her, talk with her, and explain why he'd ghosted her.

"Yo, Fraser!" Myles called out.

"You have got to be fucking kidding me," Ash muttered, putting on a fresh CPD t-shirt. He turned and watched Myles and Zain approach.

"Where you headed to?" Zain asked, leaning against the opposite lockers.

"Away from you motherfuckers," Ash joked. He may have smiled but he was serious. He'd just spent four entire days with his team doing exhausting work. He needed a little break. Even if it was twelve hours. He'd take it.

"Don't tell me you're running from hard work." Myles barked a laugh.

Both of them looked as if they were fresh from the showers as well. Ash eyed them and released a snort.

"Well, if you must know, I'm going to go pick up Deana," he admitted.

Their laughs filled the air. He stuffed his foot in his boot and flipped them both off.

"The pretty teacher got you wrapped around her little finger." Myles snickered, slapping Ash on the back.

"Whatever." He shook his head. Hell, Ash didn't care who knew he had the hots for Deana. He just prayed him not returning her call wouldn't be a turn-off for her.

Dating a SWAT officer was hard.

Loving one, damn near impossible.

It would take a strong woman to be in a committed relationship with a SWAT officer.

"I'm just fucking with you, man. She's a good woman." Myles folded his arms in front of his massive chest while watching Ash tie up his boots. "So what do you have planned?"

"No clue," Ash declared. He was running on pure adrenaline at the moment. All he knew was he would pick her up from work and then he'd figure it out.

"Ash, the lover boy." Zain snorted. "Why don't you take her out for happy hour at that brewery down on Bluff Road. I hear they have some great food, plenty of beer choices, and today should have a live band."

Ash turned with a raised eyebrow to Zain who shrugged.

"Hell, that sounds good. I may have to check it out, too." Myles sighed, rubbing a hand along his bald head.

"Why don't we all meet down there? Mac and Dec can bring the girls. Ash can bring his girl. It could be fun," Zain said, pushing off the lockers.

Ash nodded, thinking it would be nice for Deana to meet the rest of the team. Sarena and Aspen could explain to her about being with a guy who was a member of SWAT.

He didn't want to mess up whatever this was between them.

"Yeah, I'll grab Deana, and we'll meet you down there. About five?" He glanced down at his watch. School would be getting out soon, and he wanted to make sure he got there before she left. He grabbed his duffle bag and slammed the locker shut.

"I'll go tell Mac and Dec now. Not going to get my ass handed to me twice," Myles muttered, turning to leave.

Ash snorted. At least someone was thinking straight.

"I'll let the rest of the team know," Zain offered.

They followed Myles out of the locker room with

Ash headed toward the back doors where his car was parked. He jogged down the stairs and beelined straight to his car.

He just hoped that Deana was ready to officially start dating Ashton Fraser.

10

Ash walked through the bustling hallway. He dodged the students who were rushing from their classrooms. He remembered that same feeling when he was younger. There was nothing better than that feeling of getting out of school and having the weekend off.

He smiled at a few of the kids and gave a couple high fives before he arrived at Deana's classroom. He stepped inside the doorway and found her bent down putting books onto a shelf.

He gaze went even lower and took in her feet.

Her heels were back.

God, I love her in heels.

His gaze dropped down to her ass on display, and a stirring shifted below his belt.

"Someone must be feeling better," he said.

She screamed and tumbled to the floor. Laughing, she turned and looked at him over her shoulder. "Ash!"

"Hey, I don't think you are supposed to be on the

floor." He chuckled, jogging across the room to her. He held his hand out for her. "I mean, if you want me close to you, I can think of other things we can do down there."

"Watch it, one of the kids may hear you," she scolded. Her small hands slipped into his.

He gently pulled her up and wrapped his arm around her waist, holding her against him. She leaned into his embrace, and her smile faltered.

"Where have you been? I thought you were avoiding me or something."

"Never that." He shook his head and gripped her tight. He reached up and caressed her cheek. "I've literally been at work since I left your place."

"Really?" she gasped. Her eyes widened. She rested her hand on his chest and blew out a deep breath. "Wow. I couldn't even begin to imagine. Eight hours with my kids here and I'm ready to go crazy." She laughed.

"Yeah, believe me, I was going crazy. I'm dead on my feet and off tonight. I couldn't wait to see you again," he admitted. He skimmed his thumb over her face and trailed it down to her lips.

"Please tell me whatever you were doing was safe," she murmured. Fear rose in her eyes, and a small smile played on his lips.

"Then it's best I don't tell you." He pressed a soft

kiss to her mouth. He didn't want her to have to worry about his job or the fact that no part of being a SWAT officer was safe. She leaned into his body, and as much as he wanted the kiss to go further, he had to remember they were still at the school. "Do you have any plans now?"

"I don't think so," Deana said, stepping back from him.

"Good. You're coming with me. We can leave your car and come back for it later." He grinned.

"Where to?" She moved away and strolled to her desk.

His eyes dropped down, and he caught the sway of her hips. He bit back a groan at his cock pushing against his jeans. She gathered items and threw them in her bag.

"The guys are meeting up down at the brewery down on Bluff Road."

"Oh, I've heard good things about that place." She swung her bag on her shoulder and grabbed her keys. She walked over to him with a small smile. "So is this an official date, Officer Fraser?"

He seized her by her neck, unable to resist stealing a kiss.

"Yeah, Miss Dawson. We are officially dating." He chuckled, entwining their fingers. It felt good to say the words. He had been lusting after Deana

Dawson for so long, it was time he made her his woman

After locking up her classroom, they quickly made it out of the school. He guided her toward his car in the parking lot. Opening the door for her, he assisted her inside the vehicle. He jogged around the car and hopped in the driver's seat.

"So who all will be there?" Deana asked, shifting in her seat to face him.

He turned the car on and pulled off. He glanced over at her and found her eyes wide with curiosity.

"My entire team should be there—"

"I'll be the only woman hanging out with—"

"No." He laughed, cutting her off.

Horror lined her face before she relaxed. "Oh good." She blew out a deep sigh and leaned back in her seat.

"Myles will be there. You've already met him. My two sergeants will be there. Mac is bringing his wife, Sarena, and Dec is bringing his fiancée, Aspen. Brodie, Zain, and Iker may be riding solo." He coasted the car to a red light and braked.

Grabbing her hand, he pulled it up to his lips and brushed a soft kiss to her skin. Ash was rewarded with a soft smile.

"Don't get a big head, but I did miss you," she whispered. Her gaze drifted down to his shirt.

Ash chuckled. "I missed you, too. I hated that I had to leave that night. I would have given my right arm to finish what we started."

His smile slowly faded. Deana's gaze flickered back up to his. He reached for her and gripped her chin between his fingers, drawing her closer.

"Really?" She whimpered.

"Yeah, really." He leaned over and brushed his lips against hers. A slight moan slipped from her. He pressed another kiss to her lips. "I wanted to feel you wrapped around my cock when you came."

Deana closed the small gap between them. Their mouths merged in a hard kiss. He thrust his tongue forward, sweeping into her mouth. Her hand rested on the side of his face as the kiss deepened. Deana's tongue stroked his, urging him duel with hers.

Fleeting thoughts of turning the car around and heading to his place crept into his mind.

They could take a rain check with the guys.

He needed to have Deana spread out underneath him. Just thinking of slipping inside her warm cocoon had his dick straining against his jeans, demanding to be let out.

A blaring car horn behind them had them breaking apart.

Ash released a curse. He waved a hand to the car behind the and pushed his foot on the gas.

"Jesus," Deana whispered.

He glanced over at her and found her just as shaken by the kiss as he was.

He pushed harder on the gas.

"One drink," he muttered.

"No more than two." She snorted. "We wouldn't want to be rude since we can't stay long."

His gaze flickered to hers, and a grin spread across his face.

She'd read his mind.

He nodded, not going to disagree. "Yes, ma'am."

Two drinks, and then he was taking Deana home to finish what they'd started.

Deana couldn't stop laughing. Sarena and Aspen were amazing women. They immediately made Deana feel welcome in the restaurant with the men. Sarena had shared with them how she and Mac used to be neighbors and how they'd met.

She wiped the tears from her cheeks at the story of Mac asking her on a non-date date.

When Deana had been introduced to him, he seemed so hard and rigid, unlike Ash's easygoing personality.

"So enough about us." Sarena patted Deana's hand. A slick smile spread across her face.

Deana recognized the look as one her kids give her when they were scheming.

"How did you meet Ash?"

Aspen took a sip of her wine and raised an eyebrow. "Yes, please do tell."

Deana glanced over at the men. They were a tall, muscular group and all alphas. She instantly picked up on the bond they shared. Currently, they were surrounding an arcade game where they were using a fake gun to kill zombies. They were relaxed and smiling while they talked crap to each other.

"He's the DARE officer at the school where I teach. So I've known him for a while. It was just recent we decided to act on what we feel is between us," she sheepishly admitted. She reached for her drink and downed it.

"Don't be embarrassed." Sarena waved her hand nonchalantly. "Let me be the first to tell you that Marcas may be a badass with his men and out in the streets, but when he comes home, he's a doting husband. He'd do anything for me." Her eyes drifted off while her smile faltered slightly. She paused as if reliving something in her past.

"Are you okay?" Deana asked, reaching out to cover her hand with hers.

Sarena blinked a few times before nodding. She peered over her shoulder. Deana took notice of the heated look that was exchanged between the married couple.

"Dec and Mac are best friends. They served in the Navy together. I can agree, they are all pure alpha men who fall hard." Aspen smiled. "Ash is a good man. Their team is extremely close, and they'd do anything for each other."

"Yeah, anything," Sarena agreed.

The two women shared a glance, and Deana was left with the feeling as if she were missing something.

"Maybe it's the drinks, but I feel as if there is something you guys aren't telling me," Deana blurted out. She was on her fourth, maybe fifth drink. She'd stopped counting long after the last round.

She blinked.

Had it been five or six?

She giggled.

"Well, both of us had some problems, and the guys banded together to help us," Aspen said. She glanced down at her hand before looking up at Deana.

Deana instantly sobered, feeling the conversation turning serious.

"What kind of problems?" she asked.

"Oh, you know...the kind where I got kidnapped by some gangsters who were trying to get back at

Marcas," Sarena admitted, taking a long sip of her drink.

Deana's mouth dropped open at Sarena's admission.

Kidnapped?

Holy hell.

"I was in protective custody and almost killed," Aspen muttered, finishing her wine off. "Ashton was right there to help save me. Hell, all of them were."

Deana glanced over and caught Ash leaning against the game. Their eyes connected, and her heart skipped a beat. She knew they had originally agreed for a couple of drinks then would leave, but they'd ended up having too much fun with the group.

He tossed her a wink then turned back to the guys. Myles wrapped an arm around his shoulders, and they walked off out of her sight.

"Their jobs are really that dangerous?" she asked. She knew she had to sound naïve, but she didn't want to think of Ash's life in danger while he was at work. She'd watched movies and television shows that depicted cops and SWAT, but she didn't want to think his job was like those.

"Extremely," Aspen replied, her voice hollow.

It sent a shiver down Deana's spine to think that Ash could be killed in the line of duty.

Aspen reached for an appetizer that was on the

table and popped it into her mouth. "They're the good guys, but to the bad guys, they're the wrong guys."

"I'm not sure if you are going to be getting serious with Ash, but we both can vouch that he's one hell of a man," Sarena said.

She'd always observed the way he was with the kids at the school. She could see he loved being around them and showing them that cops were the good guys. The boys, Chip and Lucas, looked up to him and talked about him nonstop for days after his visit to the school.

Deana didn't need to be told twice that Ash was a good man.

She knew it deep down.

"How do you live with the fear that they may not walk back through the door at night?" she asked. Her stomach flipped at the thought of never seeing Ash again.

Sarena and Aspen glanced at each other. Deana could see the two women shared a bond between them.

"You never let them know you have the fear of them never returning," Aspen answered.

Deana's eyebrows shot up high. She nodded before turning her attention to Sarena who shrugged.

"You love them hard and good every day as if it's their last."

11

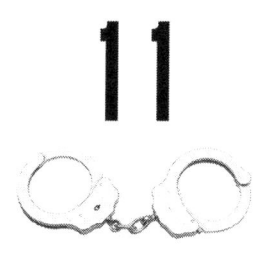

Ash turned off the sink and reached for a paper towel. He dried his hands and glanced at himself in the mirror. This night had turned out better than he'd hoped. Sarena and Aspen had taken Deana right in under their wings.

They'd stayed past their two-drink agreement, but now it was time for them to leave. He was sure the guys would understand.

He tossed the balled-up paper into the trash and left the restroom.

"Officer Fraser," an unfamiliar voice called his name.

Ash's muscle grew tense. Warning sirens blew in the back of his head.

He turned and glanced at the strange man standing by the back door.

"Who wants to know?" He crossed his arms in

front of his chest, unafraid. He had about twenty pounds of muscle on the guy.

His hard eyes stared at Ash. His dark hair was cropped close to his head. Tattoos lined his arms that were on display by his sleeveless shirt.

Ash couldn't place him.

"My name doesn't matter." The man snickered.

"I'm done here," Ash snapped. He spun on his heel and headed toward the main area of the restaurant. It was definitely time for them to go.

"That woman of yours is awfully pretty."

Ash halted. He peered over his shoulder and narrowed his eyes on him. He immediately rotated around and made his way toward the man.

His footsteps ate up the hall quick.

Mentioning Deana was a threat.

He closed his hands into tight fists.

He stopped in front of the thug and glared into his eyes.

"I don't think I heard you from down the hall," Ash growled. Rage filled his chest as he watched man's lips curve up into a sinister grin. "What did you say?"

"Such a badass. My cousin told me what you did to him over her," the stranger sneered.

Ash held back a curse. This had to be the cousin of the idiot he'd fought at the bar.

At the moment he couldn't remember the asshat's name.

Alarms went off in Ash's head.

He caught sight of the small tattoo near the guy's eye and instantly pegged him for a member of the Demon Lords.

The gang was one of the most violent criminal organizations in South Carolina. The Demon Lords had their hands in illegal weapons, drugs, and human trafficking.

SWAT had been called in plenty of times to help the sheriff's department's Gang Unit in dealing with the gang. There was no love lost between the Demon Lords and Columbia's SWAT team.

It was the same gang that had abducted Sarena.

The same one that their SWAT team had crippled twice.

The SWAT team had helped with one of the largest raids of weapons and narcotics in their state's history, causing the gang to lose a substantial amount of money.

Not only did they cripple them financially, but it had been Declan who had made the kill shot and took the life of their leader when he'd abducted Sarena.

Ash stiffened, sensing a figure behind him. Something hard pushed into his back, and he recognized it as the barrel of a gun.

"Let's take a walk outside," a deep baritone voice ordered.

Ash released curse.

This was not good.

He raised his hands and nodded.

Fuck.

His weapon was currently locked up in the glove box in his car.

The guys would notice he was gone and would come looking for him.

"Lead the way," he murmured. He willed his heart to slow down. This was not the first time he'd had a weapon aimed at him. He glanced over his shoulder and took in the scowling face of the thug behind him. He stood taller than Ash by an inch or so and was pretty stocky.

He followed the first guy out the back door. Ash took notice that the fire alarm did not go off when Tattoo Face went through it.

The door shut behind them with a small click. Ash's eyes immediately focused out in the dark alley. There were two other men waiting for them—one was the guy from the bar.

"Gus, this is him?" Tattoo asked.

The guy nodded.

Ash barked a short laugh. "How's your face holding up?"

Gus narrowed his eyes on him and shook his head slowly.

"Gus here suffered a broken jaw," Tattoo sneered. "Had to get his jaw wired shut. He's been having to eat his food through a fucking straw thanks to you."

"Hopefully he learned his lesson," Ash snapped. His gaze flickered around, taking in the men moving closer to him. His muscles tensed. He may not be able to take on the three of them, but he'd damn sure make sure he did damage.

"That's what we're about to do to you," the third man warned, stepping closer. He was tall with long, thin hair pulled back in a low ponytail. He cracked his knuckles, and his scowl deepened. "You cops think that you can just do what you want to do."

"Who was looking out for my cousin the night you attacked him?" Tattoo snapped.

The men circled around Ash while Gus looked on.

"I didn't attack anyone," Ash scoffed. He found it funny that Gus had been such the big man at the bar and now he was having his cousin's gang members teach him a lesson. "You want to get revenge, come fight me like a man."

"Nah, we got this," Tattoo said.

The men converged on Ash.

He threw a punch first, connecting with Tattoo's face. A solid fist landed over Ash's kidney. He grimaced, turning and swinging at Ponytail. Ash's fist connected with Ponytail's stomach, but he received another punch to the other side of his back.

He'd be damned if he went out without them getting a scratch.

He fought hard, landing punches and kicks on the three thugs. They fought dirty. Something hard slammed against Ash's back, sending him down on his knees.

"Take this as a warning," Tattoo growled. His foot landed on Ash's stomach, knocking the wind out of him. They continued to kick and beat Ash down. He tried to protect his head and his body. "The Demon Lords never forget."

Kicks and hits kept coming.

Ash released a grunt, trying to get up. He got to his knees once more, but something hard and flat landed on his back again, sending him falling onto the ground.

He released a curse.

An image of Deana smiling in the car came to mind.

At least she's safely tucked in the restaurant with the others.

A sharp pain burst forth in his head, rendering him unconscious.

"What the fuck is taking Ash so long?" Myles muttered.

Deana glanced down at her watch and agreed. His friends had all made their way to the table, but Ash's chair next to her was empty.

"Maybe he had too much to drink." Brodie snorted, raising his glass.

"Lightweight." The guy named Iker laughed.

Worry filled Deana. One of the guys had said Ash had gone to the bathroom. It had been over fifteen minutes since the guys had sat down with her, Sarena, and Aspen.

"I'm going to go check on him," Deana announced, standing from her chair. She hefted her purse up on her shoulder.

"Myles, go with her," Mac said. He more like commanded it. His rough voice was almost a growl. His arm was wrapped around Sarena who snuggled into him.

"Sure. It's been a while since I've had to carry Ash's ass home drunk." Myles laughed, pushing back from the table.

Deana chuckled but couldn't shove down the feeling that something was wrong.

"I'm sure he's fine and I'm overreacting," she said, walking alongside Myles.

He shrugged. "It is taking him a while. Let's just make sure he's okay."

Deana nodded. She blew out a deep breath and turned down the hallway where the bathrooms were located.

"I'll stay here," she said, choosing a spot to wait for them.

"Be right back." Myles disappeared into the men's room but returned in seconds. He stepped back into the hallway with a scowl. "No one's in there."

"Then where could he be?" She didn't think they'd missed him when they'd walked away from the table.

Myles rested his hands on his waist and glanced toward the emergency door. His head tilted to the side, and Deana looked at it.

"You don't think he left, do you?" she asked. She gripped the strap of her purse tight as doubts ran through her head.

Would he just leave her?

"What?" Myles swiveled his gaze back to her. His eyebrows rose high. "Never that. He's crazy over you."

Her heart skipped a beat at the thought of Ash sharing his feelings with his friend. That gave her some relief, but still...

Where was Ash?

He stalked to the exit at the end of the hallway. It had the word 'emergency' over it.

"So if you don't think he left, why are you checking a door?" she asked, strolling behind him.

"Gut feeling. Something's off," Myles muttered. He pushed it open.

She was expecting a loud alarm to blare, but it never came.

"Isn't it supposed to alarm?"

"Yeah." He pushed it open farther and stepped outside. His curses filled the air, and he disappeared into the night.

She dashed to the door and froze.

Myles was kneeling next to a body that was lying on the ground.

Ash.

A strangle cry escaped her.

"Ash!" She rushed over to him and fell to her knees. Her heart slammed against her chest.

Was he alive?

Myles gently rolled him over onto his back.

A groan escaped Ash's lips. Deana reached out a hand and brushed his hair back from his face.

"Ash, can you hear me?" she whispered. Her hand shook as she pulled it away.

"Deana?" He moaned.

She gathered him to her, not caring she was kneeling on the ground in a back alley. She couldn't care less what was getting on her clothes.

"What the hell happened?" Myles demanded, pulling his phone from his pocket. His voice was deep and laced with the fury that was on his face. He stood and looked around.

Deana was glad that she wasn't on his bad side.

"Fuckers beat the shit out of me." He groaned. His face was darkened with what Deana was sure to be bruises.

"Hey, I found Ash," Myles announced to whoever he called. "We got a problem."

Deana's vision blurred with tears. She gathered Ash closer to her. His body stiffened, and she paused.

"Did I hurt you?" she asked, her voice ending on a squeak.

"Are you okay?" He turned his face to her.

In the low light she could see one eye was almost swollen shut.

"Don't worry about me. I'm not the one who just got the shit kicked out of him," she murmured.

"You think I look bad, you should see what they look like," he tried to joke but ended with a grimace.

"This is not the time to try to joke, Ash." She barked a short laugh. Only Ash would try to get her to smile and laugh while he laid in pain.

The door flew open, and footsteps filled the air. She turned to see Mac, Declan, and the other guys right behind them filing out into the alley.

"Ash, what the hell happened?" Declan asked, kneeling beside them.

"Shit." Ash gasped. His eye closed briefly, and he muttered something.

"What did you say?" Deana asked, unsure she had really heard him.

"I knew we should have left after the second drink," he repeated.

A giggle burst from her. She couldn't help it and didn't care that the guys were staring at her as if she'd lost her marbles.

Yeah, they should have left after their agreed two-drink minimum.

12

"I can walk." Ash cursed, stepping through the door to his home. This was not the way he'd imagined bringing Deana to his house for the first time.

"If you need me, I can carry you."

Ash's gaze swiveled to Myles who stood behind him with a smirk.

"The fuck you will." Ash snorted.

He'd spent all night at the hospital and refused to stay longer. The sun was finally up, and the doctors had agreed to release him.

"I got him, Myles," Deana said, walking through the door.

Ash leaned against the wall, refusing to look weak. Hell, he may have taken a beating, but there was no way he'd let it put him on his ass for more than a few hours.

He was Ashton Fraser.

That beating was nothing.

He shifted his arm, and his ribs screamed in protest.

The scans at the hospital had revealed a few cracked ribs.

Nothing that wouldn't heal with a little time.

"Well, if he gives you trouble, call me." Myles chuckled.

Ash flipped his middle finger at his friend. Deana came to him and slid an arm around his waist. He held back a grimace, not wanting her to move away from him.

She'd been by his side the entire night. The dark areas beneath her eyes revealed that she hadn't gotten any sleep at all in the emergency room.

"There won't be a need," Ash murmured, bringing her closer. Cracked ribs be damned. He needed to feel Deana against him.

"We're going to need to talk after you get some sleep. Me and the guys know there is more than the robbery gone wrong bullshit you gave the cops." Myles crossed his arms in front of his chest. He narrowed his eyes on Ash.

"We're going to handle this personally," Ash said. He hadn't told the officers who had visited the hospital to take his report. Ash and his men would take care of the Demon Lords.

Myles nodded, satisfied with the answer.

"Let me get some rest and food. Tomorrow, I'll be a new man, and we'll get everyone together to talk."

"I'll let Mac and Dec know," Myles replied. He leaned forward and squeezed Ash on his shoulder, turning to Deana. "Take care of him."

"I will." Deana smiled.

Myles tipped his head to them before leaving out the front door. It closed with a slight click.

"I thought he'd never leave," Ash muttered.

"Ash!" Deana gasped.

He tried to crack a smile, but his damn swollen eye prevented it. "Come on. Let me show you around—"

"No, point me in the direction of your bedroom so I can help you get there." Deana laughed.

"Slow down, woman!" he teased her.

She rolled her eyes at him. They leisurely began the walk through the living room toward the stairs.

"We've only had our first date last night, and you're already trying to get me to the bedroom?"

"Ashton Fraser! You know that's not what I meant," she sputtered, tightening her grip on him.

His legs felt like mush, but he refused to lean on her fully. He outweighed her and was much taller than her. They slowly made their way up the stairs, and he directed her to the master suite.

He pushed the door open to his bedroom and limped across to the bed. He let out a groan, sitting on the edge of it. Deana knelt before him and tossed her purse on the bed. She pulled off his shoes and socks.

"I've envisioned you taking my clothes off multiple times, but I can honestly say, never did I imagine it would be under these circumstances."

Deana's eyes flew to his. She smiled from her position. Even with the slight smudges of dirt on her face, she was the most beautiful thing he'd ever seen. Her hands slid up along his thighs, and a stirring flickered between his legs.

"I know." She sighed. "You took care of me when I was hurt, and now it's time for me to repay the favor."

She stood from the floor and helped him take his shirt off. He bit back a moan when he had to raise his arms to allow her to slide the shirt over his head.

"Shit," he uttered with a wince. The pain was a shooting, piercing stab that took his breath away. He glanced down at his chest and took in his normal tan skin marred with large black and blue bruises.

"Here, I have the medication from the pharmacy," she said, reaching for her purse.

"I don't need pills."

"It will not hurt your tough guy image to have one. It will take the edge off, and with those ribs, you're going to be in pain for days." She arched a perfectly sculpted eyebrow. He stared at her, and she returned his stare. "You swallow the pill, and I'll get in the shower with you."

He held out his hand without argument.

Deana Dawson in the shower with him.

Naked.

He'd swallow the entire bottle to watch water slide along her curves.

"Give me the damn pill, woman," he growled.

She chuckled and placed one in his hand. "Come on, big guy. Let's get you washed up."

Deana switched the water on and waited. She tested it out, and when it was finally manageable, she turned back to Ash. She froze in place, finding him standing behind her with his jeans and briefs in a puddle on the floor.

She took in his well-muscular chest and well-defined abs. Her heart raced as her gaze continued its journey farther down and connected with the long length of his cock hanging between his legs.

Her core pulsed at the sight of it.

Her gaze flew up and met Ash's one good eye. A smirk lingered on his lips, and she knew she had been caught ogling his goods.

"Is the water ready for me?" he asked.

Unable to speak, she nodded.

He limped past her and into the shower stall. His house was beautiful from what she'd seen of it. It was in a quiet neighborhood tucked away at the end of the street. He had a large piece of land with the gorgeous house placed on it.

His bedroom was decorated in dark masculine colors, and his en suite was modern with a standalone shower, a tub, and his-and-hers sinks.

She blinked a few times, trying to gather her thoughts.

She swiveled around and watched Ash stand underneath the showerhead.

"You said if I took that pill, you'd be getting in with me," Ash said, facing her.

"That I did." She didn't think he'd actually go for her bribe. Why she'd made that one, she didn't know. The words had escaped her mouth before they were processed by her brain.

But seeing him underneath the spray of water, naked, had her stripping her clothes off fast.

Shyness crept into her chest at the thought of the extra pounds she carried, but one look into Ash's heated gaze and those self-doubts disappeared.

Deana walked around the glass wall and didn't even care about getting her short curls wet.

All she could think of was standing next to Ash to get a close look at him.

"The water is perfect," he murmured as she stepped near him.

The warm water caressed her skin. She couldn't look away from Ash.

"Just as you are."

Her heart skipped a beat. She grabbed soap on the marble shelf and focused her attention on him. With his aches and bruising there was no way he'd be able to wash himself properly.

"Looks like you need my help, Ashton," she teased.

Ash's eye darkened with him apparently understanding her meaning. She lathered up her hands with the soap and ran one along his pectoral muscle.

His sharp intake of breath met her ears. Her hands continued on their journey. She was careful around the many dark areas marring his skin, trying not to cause him any more discomfort.

"Deana," he breathed.

They made their way to his erected penis. Ash fell back against the wall behind him. She slid her hand along his length. It was hard yet soft. She circled his mushroomed tip and glanced up at him.

His one good eye was on her. His chest was rising and falling fast.

She felt empowered by the way he was apparently

affected by her. This tough, SWAT officer trembled from her touch.

"Ash," she murmured, tightening her grip on him while she continued to stroke him. Her gaze wandered back down to his thick length. Licking her lips, she knelt on the floor before him.

"Deana, you don't have to do this," he gasped. His hand was braced on the wall while the other rested on her shoulder.

"I want to," she whispered. The warm water continued to spray on her back like a gentle massage. She tilted her head back and met his gaze while guiding the head of his cock between her lips.

She sucked it in, and it tore a groan from him. She slid her tongue along his length and relished the taste of him. She pulled back and bathed the tip with her tongue and on the underside of it.

She trailed her hand along his hard shaft, and it ripped a moan from her. Deana gasped, her core pulsing. She ached to feel Ash stretch her, pushing deep inside her, but for now, it was her turn to pleasure him.

"Deana." His strangled moan was enough to fuel her on.

He was too large for her to take him all the way, so she had to be clever. She stroked the length of him as she sucked on his fully engorged cock.

His hips moved, pushing his length farther inside

her mouth. She relaxed her jaw and throat to allow him to thrust forward.

It felt good knowing that it was her causing him to writhe around from the pleasure. She wanted to see him fall apart just as he had made her do.

Deana couldn't take her eyes off the big, strong man before her. With his eye closed, he leaned his head back on the tile and allowed her to have her way with him.

She quickened her pace.

His fingers made their way to her hair and entwined themselves in her wet curls, anchoring her in place.

His hips moved faster.

Ash's grunts grew louder as she sucked him deeper to the back of her throat. The sound of her name on his lips had her gut clenching with anticipation of what was going to come later.

Using her other hand, she gently caressed his heavy sac.

"Fuck!" he cursed. His body shook, but Deana kept going. "I'm about to come, Deana."

She looked up and knew what he was asking.

She tightened her grip on his shaft and gave another tug at his scrotum, and he let out a shout.

She accepted his release, swallowing his salty essence.

Ash fell back against the wall, out of breath. She let go of his semi-soft cock and gave it one last lick.

Deana looked up at Ash and took notice of his pale color. His chest was rising fast, and a grimace of pain flashed across his face.

"Oh God!" she cried out, scrambling from the floor. She turned and shut the water off. Her heart pounding, she gripped his arm and wrapped it over her shoulder to help hold him up. Ash falling to the floor was the last thing she needed. How would she explain she was giving Ash head and he fell over on the floor after climaxing? Even she knew Myles would never let Ash live that down. "Are you okay? Do you need more of your pain medication?"

His good eye opened, and a ghost of a smile flashed.

"Baby, that was the best medicine no doctor can prescribe."

13

Ash slowly opened his eye. A small smile rested on his lips as he thought of the horror that had crossed Deana's face in the shower. As much pain as he was in, it had faded the minute she'd knelt on the floor before him.

The pain had been long forgotten the second his dick had slipped between Deana Dawson's sweet lips.

He'd never seen anything as beautiful as his cock disappearing into her lush mouth.

His shaft stirred beneath the covers with him just remembering their shower together.

His smile faded at the thought of the pain rushing back for him the second he'd orgasmed.

It had slammed into him, taking his breath away. He remembered his legs growing weak and him falling back against the tile wall.

It was all worth it.

What he had said was true.

Deana had given him the best medicine that no doctor could prescribe.

Jesus, that woman's mouth was dangerous.

She had fussed over him and marched him directly to bed. She'd made him take another pain pill and tucked him in.

He didn't even get to say two words before finding himself underneath the covers.

Speaking of Deana, where the hell was she?

Peeking at the alarm clock on his nightstand, he froze.

He'd slept a good long while.

He stared over at the window, and it appeared as if the sun was setting.

Next to the clock was his pain pill bottle and a glass of water.

Reaching for them, he took one pill and downed it with some water.

"Welcome back to the land of the living," Deana's southern drawl caught his attention.

He glanced at the door. She stood there with a small smile and a plate of food in her hand.

What really caught his attention was the fact she was wearing one of his CPD t-shirts. Her bare legs peeked out from the hem that stopped near her knees. Her red hair was now contained in two braids, giving her a more youthful appearance. Her face was void of any makeup, and he honestly preferred her au naturel.

She had a natural beauty to her, and it made him even more attracted to her.

"Hey there yourself," he greeted her. He made to sit up but grimaced from the pain in his ribs.

"Be careful." She rushed across the room. She set the plate down on the table and moved to help him.

"I got it," he muttered. There was no way she'd be able to lift him up without hurting herself. He struggled but was finally able to sit up and rest back against the headboard. "What have you got there?"

"I hope you don't mind me going through the kitchen," she began shyly.

He peered at her through his one decent eye. She looked good wearing his t-shirt, walking through his house. He would have loved to see her snooping through the kitchen and cooking in his shirt. Just the thought of her cooking for him had his heart racing.

"No, not at all. Make yourself comfortable," he murmured.

"Well, since you were sleeping so soundly, I made us some breakfast." She chuckled.

"One of my favorite meals is breakfast for dinner," he admitted.

"Really?" Her face brightened as she sat on the edge of the bed.

The smells greeting him crushed his stomach to announce that it had been since last night when he'd last eaten.

"Yes. When we were younger and my parents got home late from work, my mom would cook me and Gizzy breakfast for dinner. It was always a hit."

"Your sister's name is Gizzy?" Deana asked, tilting her head to the side.

"Yeah, short for Giselle."

"Beautiful name," Deana said.

"Sausage, biscuits, and gravy?" He moaned, reaching for the plate.

She laughed and handed it to him along with a fork. Two large biscuits were smothered in sausage and gravy. Right on the two biscuits, he could see a hint of two fried eggs hidden by the gravy.

A woman after his heart.

"I hope you don't mind me just throwing this together," she said, watching him dive into the food.

"Mind?" He groaned, taking a second bite. "Hell, woman, just move right in and cook whatever you want, whenever you want."

Her laughter filled the air. "Well, I'm glad you're enjoying it."

"Wait a minute. Where did you get the biscuits from?" He paused, stuffing his face to look at her. He'd been shopping recently and remembered purchasing sausage, but he didn't have any biscuits in the house.

"I made them. From scratch. You had all the ingredients." She shrugged nonchalantly.

He did?

There was only one person who came and made sure he had certain things in his cupboard.

His mother.

He took another bite, and the biscuit was still warm and flaky. He couldn't help but shake his head.

"Where's your plate?" he asked, trying hard not to shovel the food into his mouth.

"I ate while you were sleeping. I kept this warm for you."

She smiled at him, and Ash knew he was a goner.

Beautiful woman.

Intelligent.

Sexy.

Could cook.

It was official.

Ashton Fraser had fallen in love.

He scraped the last of the food into his mouth before sitting the plate on his nightstand. He reached for the water and held back a grimace as he took a gulp.

"You're in pain." Deana's eyes narrowed on him.

"I will be for a while," he admitted. He didn't know how he was going to go to work with cracked ribs. He held back a curse knowing that meant desk duty for him until he was healed. He was surprised he hadn't heard from Captain Spook.

But then again, he was sure Mac and Dec had updated the captain.

He glanced at Deana, and his heart pounded. He reached for her hand and brought it up to his lips. He pressed a kiss to the back of her skin and let her knuckles linger on his lips.

"Thank you," he murmured.

He watched her smile fade, and Deana became serious.

"Tell me the truth, Ash. What happened in that alley?"

He hadn't given the cops at the hospital the real story. He didn't need them investigating anything. He and his men would handle the Demon Lords.

She took his hand between hers and held it tightly. Her eyes were wide as she scooted near him. He didn't want to burden her with what had happened. He would take care of it, and she'd never have to worry.

"Listen, Deana—"

"Ash, please. The truth," she whispered. She shook her head and gazed down at their entwined fingers. "Sarena and Aspen told me how dangerous your job can be. I guess if we are going to be an item, it's something I'll have to get used to."

He held back a roll of his eyes. That wasn't what he wanted the girls to share with her. Being with a SWAT officer was damn near impossible.

Mac and Declan had both proved that with the right women, it was possible to find love.

Ash knew Deana was the right woman.

"You remember that asshat, Gus?" he asked.

"He did this to you?" she gasped.

"What? Hell no!" He grimaced. There was no way Gus would have been able to do this type of damage. The ass-whooping Ash had given him proved that he couldn't handle Ash. "Somehow he knew where we were and had his cousin and two big thugs beat the crap out of me while he watched."

"Oh my! Ash, I'm so sorry," Deana whimpered. She leaned in and cupped his jaw.

He inclined into her soft touch before pulling back from her. He pressed his forehead against hers.

"I'm just glad you're all right."

"Yeah, me, too." Ash blew out a deep breath and closed his eyes. He didn't want to start out their new relationship with dishonesty.

"You and the guys are going to go after them, aren't you?" she asked quietly.

His eye flew open and met her large brown ones. Unable to speak, he nodded.

"Will you promise to kick their asses good?"

His lips spread into a wide grin.

He knew Deana was the one for him.

"Baby, they won't know what hit them after we get done with them." He bent forward and covered her lips with his.

She immediately parted hers and allowed his tongue to slip inside her mouth.

Her tongue welcomed his, and she stroked it with hers. His cock stiffened beneath the covers.

He pushed down the slight twinge of pain and reached for Deana, dragging her closer to him.

"Ash, you're hurt," she gasped, breaking away from him.

Her lips were swollen from his kisses, and his cock was rock-hard.

He needed to be inside her.

Damn the pain.

"Move the blanket, Deana."

She hesitated, worry evident on her face.

"But I don't want to be the cause of your pain," she said weakly.

"You won't." He ran a finger along her jawline.

She grabbed the comforter and pulled the coverings off him. His cock sprang free, standing proud and erect. Her eyes zeroed in on his length, and he bit back a moan at the look of hunger that crossed her face.

"Straddle me, Deana."

Her gaze flew to his. He could see the wheels in her brain turning and he didn't want her to think.

He wanted her to feel.

Ash grabbed her hand and tugged her toward him. Deana kept her gaze locked on his as she rose on the bed and tossed her leg over him. She settled down and sat on his lap facing him.

His cock brushed the curve of her plump ass, and he had to do some quick calculations to keep from exploding.

"Are you happy now?" she asked. Her voice was just shy of a whisper.

He shook his head. He slid his hands along her smooth thighs and went on a journey underneath the soft cotton shirt that covered her body.

"No." He tugged the shirt over her head and was rewarded with her naked body. He tossed the shirt onto the floor. "Now I am."

A moan slipped from her lips as he cupped her voluptuous breasts with his hands. He had large hands, and her mounds easily filled them. He tested their weight and rolled her nipples between his fingers.

"Ash," she groaned.

Hearing her call his name made his cock jump. He leaned forward and captured her breast with his lips, sliding his tongue along the pebbled bud. He sucked her nipple fully into his mouth. Her sweet skin was tasty.

Holding both of her mounds in his hands, he took his time in bathing both of them properly with his tongue.

Deana's hips shifted, and he moaned from the sensation of her ass rubbing against his dick.

He ignored the twinge of pain from his ribs.

There was going to be nothing to stop him from finally sliding home inside Deana.

Her fingers dove into his hair as he continued to suckle on her breasts.

She tugged hard until he released the breast he'd been working. She tilted his head back and slammed her mouth on his.

He instantly took over the kiss, thrusting his tongue deep inside her mouth. He slid his hands along her torso and down to her full hips. They continued on to their journey to her nice, round ass. He gripped it tight and pulled her closer to him.

Her breasts were crushed between the two of them. He angled his head to allow the kiss to deepen.

"God, Ash," she whimpered against his lips.

"Raise up and put me inside you," he practically growled.

"I don't want to hurt you." Her lips burned a trail of kisses along the scruff on his jaw.

"That's why I need you to do some of the work, baby." He released a curse when she slid her ass along the length his cock. He tightened his hands on her. The sensation felt so damn good, he couldn't help but guide her to do it again. His cock was wedged between the cheeks of her ass. If he didn't be careful, he was going to blow before even getting inside her. "Shit. Come on, Deana. Do it now."

Ash watched her rest her hands on the headboard and stand on the bed. His cock didn't need help getting erect. In her new position, she'd put her pussy directly in his face, and the scent of her arousal had his cock growing harder.

He held his cock in his hand, and she positioned herself over him. He nestled the blunt tip into her slick folds. Sweat broke out on his forehead as she slowly impaled herself onto his dick.

"Ash." His name came out in a long, drawn-out moan.

Ash couldn't breathe.

Deana's slick channel was so damn tight.

He gripped her hips and pulled her completely down on him. They both released a shout.

He was fully buried inside her. Her slick channel was warm and everything he knew it would be.

It was a perfect fit.

He was home.

"Fuck. So big," she muttered. She wrapped her arms around his neck, crushing her breasts between them.

He didn't think she realized she'd said it out loud, but he was glad she had.

It did nothing but fuel the need to pound away inside her.

It may be the alpha inside him.

Or maybe it was the distant Neanderthal relative in his family line that suddenly made him want to go caveman and pound his chest while locking Deana in his bedroom forever.

"Deana, I need you to move," he bit out through gritted teeth.

She opened her eyes, and their gazes locked.

Ash had never connected with any woman on this level before.

Without a doubt, he knew he was in love with Deana Dawson.

She rose and fell back down on his cock.

Their heavy breathing and moans filled the air. Using his hands, he helped guide her.

They set a steady rhythm.

"Ashton," she chanted repeatedly while riding him.

His orgasm was rushing toward him, and there was no way on God's green earth he was coming before her.

He slid a hand along her side and down between

them. Her body released a shudder when his thumb connected with her swollen clit.

He continued to slam her down on him. She whimpered but took everything.

"Deana, you were made to take my cock," he gasped.

"Yes," she hissed.

Her eyes were closed, and he wanted to see her beautiful brown irises.

She changed the tempo from fast and hard to long, steady strokes. Sweat slid down his face as his balls drew up.

He was captivated by the sight of Deana riding him. Her breasts swayed in the air with her movements while her hips guided her up and down on him.

He strummed her clit faster, her breath catching in her throat. Her muscles grew tight, and she was right where he wanted her.

"Come for me, Deana," he commanded.

Her eyes flashed open, and he was greeted with her dark, lust-filled gaze.

Her eyes rolled into the back of her head, and she let out a piercing cry. Her walls clamped down on him tight with her climax, sending him into a hard orgasm.

Ash roared through his release. He held Deana still, burying his cock to the hilt while he emptied himself. His breaths were coming fast, making it hard for him to breathe as he came down from the euphoric journey.

Deana's body flopped down on his. Their sweat-soaked bodies pressed against each other.

The only sound in the room was their heavy breathing.

Deana buried her face into the crook of his neck, and he just held her in his arms. He didn't dare move her. His cock was satisfied, still buried deep.

Deana was exactly where she was supposed to be, and Ash was never letting her go.

14

Ash slowly made his way through the precinct. Monday morning had come too fast. Deana had spent the entire weekend with him, nursing him to better health.

He released a curse.

He would need to get Deana a sexy nurse outfit for the next time he needed special attention.

Just the thought of her in a sexy, short white nurse's uniform with her breasts spilling out had him adjusting himself.

Hopefully, he wouldn't really be injured next time.

That morning he had swung her by her place so she could get a change of clothes and then dropped her off at the school. He knew he shouldn't be driving, but he hadn't taken a prescribed pill since the day before.

Only over-the-counter pain pills for him.

"Hey, Fraser."

Ash turned in the direction his name was called and found Officer Max Reeves headed in his direction.

"What's up, Reeves?" Ash asked.

The uniformed officer stopped next to Ash.

"We'd heard that you got roughed up this weekend. You okay?" Reeves asked.

Ash eyed the guy. Reeves had been on the force a few years, and it was well known that Reeves wanted to try out for SWAT.

"Yeah, nothing a little rest and relaxation won't heal," he replied with a tight smile. His gaze roamed the bull pen that was bustling already at nine in the morning.

"That's one hell of a black eye," Reeves noted. He sniffed and shuffled his feet. "So I hear there are going to be tryouts for SWAT soon."

And there it was. Ash bit back a grin. He glanced at Reeves and noted he appeared to be fit, but Ash wasn't sure Reeves was SWAT material.

"Yes. The trials will be soon."

"Got any advice for me?" Reeves asked, a hopeful look on his face.

"I hate to be rude, but I was headed for a meeting." Ash took a step forward. He had to find Mac or Dec.

Reeves gave him a nod. "Maybe some other time?"

"Sure."

Ash moved on. He was on a mission to meet up with his team.

The Demon Lords would pay.

This mission would be off the books.

This time, they would take the fight to them. For Ash and his men, they would have the law on their side.

That was one of the reasons Ash loved being a cop. He got the opportunity to make the world a safer place by getting the bad guys off the streets.

He turned down the hall and found Mac in the hallway on his cell phone. Mac disconnected the call and faced to him with a scowl.

"What the hell are you doing here?" Mac asked.

"Last time I checked I worked here," Ash responded.

"Last time I checked you had a few cracked ribs. The captain has granted you some days off." Mac folded his arms against his chest. The scowl didn't leave his face.

"I don't need a few days off." Ash shook his head. Sitting at home would do nothing but make him go crazy. Now if Deana didn't have to work, that may be a reason to stay at home. "It's time we had the chat. Just us."

Mac nodded and motioned for Ash to follow him.

"Let's go to the conference room. I can get everyone there in five minutes."

As Mac said, their entire SWAT team was settled in the room with the door shut. The tension was thick in the air.

Ash knew he must make one hell of a sight with his eye. The skin around it was still slightly swollen and black. It was able to open slightly. He moved slower due to his aching ribs. The bruising along his side was darker and more pronounced.

"What is discussed in this room, stays in here," Mac began. He wouldn't need to say it twice. Each man present would do anything for their SWAT brothers. It had already been demonstrated twice with Declan's and Mac's situations. They were a band of brothers, and nothing could penetrate and break their bond.

SWAT for life.

Ash glanced around, meeting the gazes of the men he trusted, his life in their hands every single day of his job.

"Friday, I went to the can and when I came out there was a man in the hallway. He knew my name." He went on to tell them how he was forced at gunpoint to leave via the doorway and into the alley.

The room was silent while he told his story.

The tension heightened.

He knew each man was already planning revenge.

Once he got to the end, no one moved.

"The Demon Lords, huh," Myles said. He ran a hand along his bald head and leaned forward, resting his elbows on his knees.

Ash instantly knew his friend was plotting against the gang.

"So they must not have learned the last few times we've raided them."

"They must have forgot we took out their boss." Iker gave a sarcastic chuckle.

Declan had made that kill shot when the gangster, Silas Tyree, the leader of the Demon Lords, had kidnapped Mac's wife.

"How many times must we go for them before they learn?" Zain asked.

"My old man used to say, a hard head makes a soft behind." Brodie shrugged.

"This operation would be off the books," Declan announced.

"It could get dirty," Ash murmured, leaning back in his chair. He blew out a deep breath. They could get in trouble for using their resources to go after the Demon Lords.

And Gus, he was going to get his, too.

"What's new?" Iker chuckled.

Laughter went around. Iker was right.

They were always going to be all in together.

And if they got in trouble, they'd all get their asses kicked by the captain together.

SWAT for life.

Brothers in blue.

They would always bleed blue for each other. Ash's chest swelled, but he knew he didn't need to say anything else to his men.

They'd just bust his balls.

"So what's first?" Zain asked.

"First, we're going to have Ash identify the men from the alley. They are the first we go after," Mac said. He was the leader of their team. When he spoke, everyone listened. "We're going after everyone in their organization."

"They won't know what hit them," Myles said, clapping his hands together. His excitement spread throughout the room. Myles had a way about him that everyone wanted to push themselves as hard as he pushed forth on missions. "I'm assuming we're going to bring in the Gang Unit."

"Yeah, I'm going to call in a favor to Cameron. I'm sure he'll be all too happy to give us a few things to clean up for them," Declan stated.

They had worked with the sheriff department's Gang Unit before on plenty of occasions. Murmurs filled the air.

The door flew open, and all side conversations halted as Captain Spook strode through the door.

Shit.

His hard gaze swept over everyone and landed on Ashton.

"What the hell is going on in here?" Captain Spook demanded.

Mac stood up straighter. His face was void of all emotion.

"We were just going over tasks for this week," Mac replied without a hitch.

"Do you think I was born yesterday, Sergeant MacArthur?" Spook demanded. His eyes narrowed on Mac before sweeping back over the others.

No one volunteered any information.

"I know you all are up to something. Fraser landed in the emergency room Friday night, and come Monday morning, my SWAT team is having an unannounced meeting for weekly fucking tasks."

Everyone remained quiet. Ash wiped his face of any emotion. Spook was a smart man. He didn't get to where he was in his career on his good looks. He was one smart cop, and even though he wasn't still out in the field, he was still sharp. Ash, like everyone else, stared straight ahead and didn't say a word.

"Captain, I assure you, nothing is going down," Mac replied.

Spook glared at the sergeant, and had Mac been a lesser man, he wouldn't have been able to hold the stare.

"Don't let me find out you're planning something. It will be your asses on the line. I will not bail you out." He turned on his heel and paused at the door. His icy stare stopped on Ash. "Fraser."

"Yes, sir?" Ash already knew what was coming. He was sure he just made a pleasant sight with his black-and-blue bruises lining his face.

"Mac updated me on the extent of your injuries. You were to take a few days off, but since your stubborn ass is here, it's desk duty until you're cleared by the physician. Any negotiations, they'll be done from the truck."

"Yes, sir." Ash wasn't going to argue with the captain. One wrong move, and his ass could be busted down to traffic duty. Just the thought of walking the streets and issuing parking tickets had a shudder passing through his spine.

The door shut behind the captain.

Ash's gaze wandered around the room, and he let out the breath he didn't realize he'd been holding.

"Dec," Mac murmured.

"Calling him now," Declan shot back with his phone to his ear. He stood and moved to the corner.

"So, one thing I want to know," Myles announced.

Ash focused his attention on him. "How did they know you were there Friday night?"

"No clue." Ash shrugged.

"We were in the locker room making the plans. Anyone could have heard us," Zain added.

"But who in the locker room of the police station would be telling a member of the Demon Lords where we'd be going out after hours?" Myles asked.

"That's a good fucking question," Mac concurred. His scowl deepened.

Ash paused and thought about it. Myles was right. It was one thing to be making plans in the station and employees would have overheard them, but who the fuck would be giving information on their whereabouts?

The leak.

Ash glanced around, and everyone was apparently thinking along the same lines.

This just went to prove there was a leak in the department.

Someone had given the Demon Lords Mac's name as the shooter of their leader's cousin.

Someone had leaked Aspen's location when the feds had her hidden in a safe house. It had never been determined if it had been the Feds or their department.

This shit had to come to an end now, before someone got killed.

"Tomorrow, are you going to play kickball with us?" Chip asked, coming to stand next to Deana's desk. "Officer Fraser said we'd have a rematch."

Deana paused and gave a soft smile to Chip. A few other boys came to stand next to him. They all looked up to Ashton, and she didn't know how to break it to them.

"Well, guys, you know Officer Fraser is a member of SWAT?" she began.

"Yeah. He's a total badass," Lucas remarked.

The kids paused and glanced at him before falling into a fit of giggles and scoffs.

She smiled and shook her head. She had to agree with the kid. "Language, Mr. Thomas, or off to the principal's office you'll go."

"I'm sorry, Miss Dawson," Lucas mumbled. His eyes brightened as he turned to his friends. "My mom let me watch this show about real life SWAT cops, and they were shooting and arresting the bad guys."

Deana wasn't sure if that type of show was appropriate for his age, but she wasn't going to argue that now.

"Yes, Officer Fraser's job is very dangerous. He and his team help ensure we are safe," she said, gaining their attention. "But Officer Fraser won't be here tomorrow. He got hurt this weekend."

The room fell silent. She looked up at the kids who were putting their stuff away before the dismissal bell pealed.

"Is he going to be okay?" Chip asked.

Deana immediately regretted telling them, but she was sure Ash wouldn't mind.

The kids surrounded her desk.

She stood from her chair. "Okay, have a seat, and I'll update you."

The kids scrambled to their desks. Deana glanced over at the clock and saw she had about two minutes until the bell rang.

She walked around her desk and leaned back against it. The one time she had the attention of every child and she wasn't teaching.

"Officer Fraser was attacked Friday night."

"He's not dead—"

"No!" Dana held up her hands, cutting off the train of thought. "No, he's fine. He's just sore and bruised up. He should be back soon. If he did come, he wouldn't be able to have fun with you kids."

Mikey Timmons raised his hand.

"Yes, Mikey?" She pointed to him.

"Him and his cop friends are going to go get them, right?" he asked.

Nods went around the room, and Deana held back a chuckle.

Bloodthirsty ten-year-olds.

"Officer Fraser and his team are the best at what they do, and they won't stop until these bad guys are off the streets."

That seemed to satisfy the kids. Another hand flew in the air.

"Yes, Mindy?" Deana called on the small girl in the front of the classroom just as the bell rang.

"Is Officer Fraser your boyfriend?"

15

Ash stood on his porch and watched Deana pull into his driveway. He grinned and hobbled down the stairs to meet her.

Today would have been his normal day of going to the school, but due to his injuries, he wouldn't have been any fun for the kids.

So he'd sent Myles instead. He was all too happy to step in. They didn't want the kids to miss out on their time with the Columbia police department. The kids were important to Ash, and having his friend go in his place meant a lot to him.

Deana stepped out of her car, and his gaze swept her curvy form.

"You have got to be the sexiest schoolteacher I've ever known," he said, opening his arms to her.

"You're just saying that," she murmured, walking into his arms. She gently wrapped her arms around his waist.

"Oh, but it's true. Mrs. Zaferopolous, my fifth-grade teacher, was nowhere as beautiful as you." He chuckled.

"Mrs. Zaferopolous?" She pulled back with a chuckle. "What kind of name is that? You are making that up!"

"I'm not. I swear!" He held his hand up, laughing. "When you meet my mother, you can ask her."

Her smile froze and began to fade. "Meet your mother?"

Ash tipped her chin up with his finger. "If you haven't guessed by now, Deana Dawson, I'm crazy over you."

"I'm crazy over you, too," she echoed with wide eyes.

He couldn't wait to take Deana over to his parents'. His mother would love everything about Deana. Bernice, better known as Bernie Fraser, was a retired teacher and would get a kick that Deana was one, too.

Unable to resist, he leaned down and pressed his lips to hers.

"Come on. I have an evening of fun planned for us," he announced. He grabbed her hand and pulled her behind him. He held back a wince of pain. He was going to fight through it as he had been doing for the last two days. He didn't like how the narcotics made him feel.

"You do?" Deana laughed, tightening her grip on his hand.

They walked up the stairs.

"I can't wait to see this."

Ash guided her into the foyer and took her sweater and hung it up in the coat closet.

"I have a night of wining, dining, games, and movies for us," he boasted.

"Games, what kind of games?" Her eyebrow rose as if she were suspicious of him. She stepped to him and used her small finger to gently poke his chest. "I just happen to know that we both are very competitive."

He grabbed her hand and brought it to his lips with a smile.

"Oh, the stakes are going to be high tonight," he promised. Her laughter did something to him. He loved hearing it and made a promise to himself to always ensure she had a smile on her face when she was not coming on his cock. "Come on, woman."

He tugged her along and stalked to the kitchen. He'd ordered out from his favorite Italian restaurant.

"Ash, this is way too much food for the two of us." She gasped, letting go of his hand. She sauntered around the oversized island and gazed at him.

"Well, for what I have planned tonight, we'll need plenty of sustenance," he joked. He scratched his head and really took a look at the spread before him.

They'd delivered enough food to feed a large army.

"Well, we can always take some for lunch and have leftovers for a few days." She giggled with a shrug. She strolled around the kitchen and stood before the double doors that led out to the patio and back yard.

"Wine?" he asked. He ambled to the end of the counter to the wine fridge that was built into the island.

"Sure." She glanced over her shoulder before returning her attention to the back yard. "I love your house, Ash. It's beautiful."

"Thanks."

When he'd bought it, he'd envisioned one day filling it with a family. It was just the right size for a growing brood, and the yard was perfect. He'd imagined taking his future sons outside and playing catch.

His breath caught in his throat at the thought. He snagged a bottle of merlot and turned to find Deana walking to him with a glass in each hand.

Ash swallowed hard.

Deana belonged in his kitchen.

In this house.

Without knowing it, he'd bought this house for her before they'd even met.

"Merlot okay?" he asked, clearing his throat.

"Yeah, that's fine." She set the glasses down on the counter. She turned and reached for the drawer where the wine opener was.

The sight of her moving around the kitchen was like a punch to the gut. He hadn't known what the future would hold, but he knew he wanted to find someone to share this house with.

Someone to settle down with and share a life with.

Deana spun around and held up the wine opener with a wide grin.

"How was Myles and the kids?" he asked. He took the opener from her and popped the cork.

She handed him a glass. He quickly poured both of them a healthy amount of wine before setting the bottle onto the island.

"Great. Now they have two cops they talk nonstop about. The kids love when you and the other cops come by. The K9 officer was a huge hit." She took a sip of her wine and leaned against the counter.

"Is that so? More so than me?" He took a small taste and reached for her with his free hand. Ash just had to have Deana in his grasp.

She giggled and rested against him, protecting her glass. "I'm sorry to burst your bubble, but German shepherd officers are way cooler with the kids."

He bent down and pressed his lips to hers for a quick kiss.

"Really?" He captured her lips again. He placed his glass down on the counter and wrapped his arms around her.

A growl escaped him as her mouth opened for him. He could taste the wine on her tongue. His cock strained against his jeans.

"Don't worry." She gasped, breaking the kiss. She reached up and trailed her fingers along his cheek. Her lips curved up into a sensual smile. "You are my favorite cop."

"Your damn right I am."

"Uno and out!" Deana yelled, slamming her cards down on the table. She danced around in her spot on the floor. Ash hadn't been joking when he'd said he had games for them to play.

It was the perfect night. Deana wasn't the type of woman who had to be taken out to fancy restaurants all the time.

Good food, wine, and a certain hot cop was enough for her.

They ate until they were full, and she'd had about three glasses of wine to his one. Even though he was on light duty, he still had to be available to be able to negotiate if he was needed for a call.

She knelt beside the coffee table where they had decided to play their vicious game of Uno.

"You're cheating," Ash grumbled, tossing his cards on the table.

She leaned forward and rested her hands on it with a wide grin.

Their game of Uno had been modified to the adult version.

Strip Uno.

"Pants off, Fraser!" She laughed.

He was left in only his jeans and underwear. She, on the other hand, was in her bra, skirt, and panties.

The bruises along his face and body were blatant reminders of the dangers of his job. She watched him slowly stand from the couch. Even with his blackened eye, he was still the sexiest man she knew.

"Yes, ma'am." His mouth tipped up in the corner. He reached for the zipper and slowly pulled it down.

She forgot to breathe when he pushed his pants down. He kicked his jeans away, leaving him in his black boxer briefs.

It should be a crime to be that muscular and sexy.

Ash's body was perfection.

His abdomen was littered with hard ridges, his biceps were well-defined, and his legs were muscular and toned. Her eyes froze on his cock. It was pressing against his briefs, creating a tent.

"Hey." His voice broke through the carnal thoughts racing through her mind. Her gaze flew to his. "Eyes up here. I'm not just a piece of meat."

She burst out laughing. He gradually sat back down on the couch and shook his head, muttering something under his breath.

Deana stood from her position and walked over to him. His bruised eye was open slightly. He watched her arrive in front of him. He leaned back on the couch with his full attention on her.

"I'm not sure I heard you. What were you muttering?" She carefully straddled him.

He released a hiss as she settled onto him. His cock strained against her bottom.

"Nothing." He shook his head. "Nothing at all, but I'm liking the direction the game is going."

"I'm going to give you one freebie to make us even," she murmured, brushing her lips over his.

"Really?" He cocked an eyebrow up in surprise.

His hands came to rest on her waist. She loved the feeling of his body next to hers. She had to be careful not to rest too much of her weight on his chest.

She pressed a soft kiss to the bruise beneath his eye. "Yes. What item of clothing would you want me to remove right now? That would make us even," she whispered.

Deana trailed kisses along his face and ended at his lips.

"Your panties," he replied without hesitation.

She smiled and pushed off the couch and stood before him. Her hands disappeared underneath her skirt, and she pulled them down. She kicked them off to the side and turned back to Ash.

"There, now we're even." She returned to her spot on his lap.

"That we are," he murmured.

Deana felt open and exposed spread out before him. Ash slid his hands underneath her skirt and gripped her ass in his large hands. He massaged her, and a moan slipped from her lips.

Her eyes fluttered shut for a brief second before reopening and focusing on Ash. His hooded eye was locked on her. Moisture seeped from between her folds.

Unable to resist, she leaned forward and kissed him.

The game was long forgotten the second her lips parted and his tongue pushed forth.

The kiss deepened, and she dug her fingers into the couch behind him. His cock brushed her bottom, and they both moaned. Her knees pushed down into the couch as she lifted herself up to get close to Ash.

She ran her fingers along his shoulders and moved them up and dove them into his soft hair.

She tore her lips from his with a gasp. "Ash."

"Fuck, Deana. I can't keep my hands off you. I swear I didn't invite you over for this," he murmured, tugging her back to him. He pressed a hard kiss to her mouth and drew back.

"I know, but I don't want to stop," she moaned, rubbing herself on his stiff length.

He reached between them and pulled his cock through the slit in his briefs. They worked together to line up the blunt tip of his cock to her opening.

She sank down on him, and they both released a groan.

He filled her as no other had before.

Her muscles contracted around him tight.

Ash's hands slid up and undid the clasp of her bra that was nestled between her breasts. He ripped the contraption from her and tossed it on the floor.

She rose and began riding her strong SWAT officer.

You love them hard and good every day as if it's their last.

Sarena's words echoed in her mind.

Their night had been perfect. He'd wined and dined her. Game night was a hit.

Now he was allowing her to take from him what she needed.

Him.

She dug her hands into the couch behind him again, anchoring her in place.

Ash's lips wrapped around her nipple and sucked it deep within his mouth. His hand held it still while he bathed the taut bud with his tongue.

Her body shook with an intense need. His other hand remained on her ass while his hips thrust forward, sending his cock deep within her core.

"Ash." His name was ripped from the depths of her soul. Her body trembled, and she felt his eyes on her. Her eyes fluttered closed from the amount of sensations flooding her.

Her orgasm was racing for her.

"Take what you need, baby," he gasped against her breast. He slid a hand between them. His fingers connected with her swollen clit and strummed the sensitive flesh.

A shudder passed through her body, and she could no longer hold back.

She threw her head back and let go. "Ash!"

His strangled cry joined hers as he held her down on him while he filled her with his release.

16

Ash leaned back on his oversized couch with Deana tucked into his side. He held her in his arms and pulled the blanket over her naked form once she went to sleep. After making love, they had laid on the couch and were watching a movie, but Deana wasn't able to hang as sleep claimed her.

Her slight snore filled the air and brought a smile to his lips.

She was sleeping so peacefully. There was no way he was going to wake her up and send her home. She'd have to spend the night at his place.

He glanced down at her and held her tight. Her dark eyelashes rested against her smooth brown skin. Her lips were plump, and he loved feeling them trailing kisses along his body.

Ash's cock stiffened, and he rolled his eyes.

"Stand down," he muttered.

He blew out a deep breath and turned his attention

back to the movie that was playing on the television, but he couldn't get into it.

The hairs on his arms rose.

Ash glanced around the dark room and didn't see anything out of the ordinary.

He tried to relax back on the couch, but the alarms in the back of his head were blaring.

He bit back a wince and slid from underneath Deana and stood. He reached for his shorts she'd hung up on the back of the couch and slid them on. He walked over to the coffee table and opened the top of the wooden table where there was a hidden compartment. He reached in and pulled his Glock from its secret place.

He had weapons stashed all over the house.

"What's wrong?" Deana's husky voice came from the couch.

He glanced at her and found her sitting up on her elbow, staring at his gun.

"It's probably nothing. Just a feeling. Throw something on," he ordered.

She nodded, sat up, and grabbed his shirt from the floor. She tossed it over her head and stood.

He strode to the windows and stared out into the darkness. The soft lights around the yard showcased the area.

Nothing was out of place.

He gripped the gun tight in his hand and flipped off the safety.

"Ash—"

He turned to her with a finger pressed to his lips. Her eyes widened, and she jerked her head in a quick nod.

Ash stalked past her and motioned for her to come to him. She ran to him, and he took her hand, pulling her behind him.

"Stay on my six," he murmured.

"Six?"

He glanced over behind him and caught the confusion in her eyes. "Directly behind me. Stay at my back."

She nodded and moved closer to him. She gripped the back of his shorts, and he was comforted having her with him.

They walked out of the family room. He aimed the gun in front of him. His ribs were aching, but he pushed the pain down.

They swept through the kitchen, the dining room, and silently made their way to the foyer in the front of the house.

His neighborhood was a quiet, safe one that had young families in it.

Little to no crime.

His gut was telling him that something was about

to go down. It had saved his life plenty of times before, and today was not the day he would ignore the warning.

This feeling wasn't one he wanted to have in his own home.

With Deana by his side, he didn't want to take a chance.

The sound of a car idling rumbled outside.

"Stay here," he murmured to Deana, leaving her at the corner of the hallway.

"But—"

He held a finger to her lips. "Stay."

Her eyes wide, she stared at him. She gave a quick jerk of her head.

He moved toward the door but jumped back as the windows of his front door shattered. Deana's scream pierced the air behind him.

He pressed himself to the wall and saw a huge rock sitting on the floor.

"What the—?" Ash rushed to the door and yanked it open. He caught sight of a figure running across his yard. Ash released a curse from the pain but ignored it as he ran down the stairs. "CPD! Freeze!" he yelled.

He jogged to the center of his yard, sweat running down his temples. He came to a halt, out of breath and, with a sharp pain radiating along his arm, raised his gun.

His hands trembled, and he lowered his weapon. There was no way he'd be hitting his target with the shakes.

The figure continued on and arrived at the car. The passenger door flew open, and he hopped in while the car's tires screeched against the road

Ash spun on his heel and stalked toward the house. He was pissed.

This was too close.

He knew without a doubt this was the Demon Lords.

They had crossed the line.

Deana was here and could have been injured. He'd go crazy if something was to happen to her.

Climbing up the stairs, he entered through the door.

"Be careful of the glass," Deana said from the hall, her voice hollow.

She peeked around the corner, and he met her gaze. He nodded before looking on the floor for the rock that had gone through the glass.

Finding the stone, he carefully stepped over glass, reaching it. A note was wrapped around it.

"What the fuck?" he muttered.

Who still threw rocks through windows with messages?

He bent down and snatched the note off the rock.

Unfolding the piece of paper, he froze. Ice spread through his veins as his gaze swept over the sheet.

Bang, bang. Officer Fraser.

You're next.

"What does it say?" Deana asked, stepping to him.

She arrived at his side, and he wrapped an arm around her.

"Don't worry about it." He folded the paper back to keep her from seeing it and pressed a kiss to her forehead.

He and the guys were going to have to make their move on the Demon Lords now.

"Ashton, I'm scared," Deana whispered. She pulled away from him with fear in her eyes.

"There's no need for you to be scared. I won't let them touch you," he assured her. He grabbed her hand and pulled her back to him. He meant every word he'd said. She would not have to live in fear for much longer.

Just for scaring his woman, Ash would make the Demon Lords pay.

That was a promise.

Deana reached out and cupped his cheek. A ghost of a smile played on her lips.

"It's not me that I'm worried about. I'm worried about you."

17

"What is this, the nineteen-sixties?" Myles chuckled, pushing the rock across the table.

With the recent events, Ash had put a call out to Myles, who in turn must have notified their entire team. Before he knew it, Mac, Declan, Brodie, Myles, Zain, and Iker were all standing around his dining room table eyeing the note and rock.

They'd even brought a few pieces of wood planks to cover the broken glass in the front door.

"I don't know, but this feels personal," Ash murmured, running a hand through his hair.

It was late, and he hadn't wanted Deana leaving his house by herself. He'd made her go and try to grab some sleep upstairs while he and his team met.

"You think?" Declan raised an eyebrow. He sat at the table and brought out his laptop. "You think you can identify the men from the brewery?"

"You bet your ass I can." Ash snorted, moving to

take the seat next to Declan. He could see their faces as if they were standing right before him. He balled his hands into tight fists just thinking of facing them again.

"Cameron sent over a file with the known associates of the Demon Lords. You pick them out, we know who to go after first," Declan announced.

"Now that's what I'm talking about," Myles said.

Murmurs echoed around the room.

"Old man Ash won't be able to roll with us injured." Brodie snickered.

"Like hell I can't," Ash snapped. He turned to Brodie with a crooked grin. "Wrap up these ribs of mine, and I'll be good as new."

The guys laughed and tossed around jokes.

He thought of how his hand had trembled when he'd aimed. He wouldn't let them know. There was no way in hell they would be going after the bad guys without him.

"Please tell me you have coffee." Zain groaned. He ran a hand along his head. "If I'm going to be here this late, I need something to help me stay awake."

"I second that." Iker gave a loud yawn.

"Kitchen. Keurig on the counter," Ash directed.

The two of them disappeared through the doorway that led to the kitchen.

"I'll think about you going out into the field. Spooks will already have our asses. I can't have you injured even more and not able to take your ass-whipping from the captain," Mac said, leaning against the table and motioning toward the computer. "Let's see if any of them are in the files."

Declan typed a few commands before turning the computer to face him. Ash pulled it in front of him and began going through the pages of criminals.

"How did Deana handle everything?" Myles asked.

Ash's gaze flickered to his for a brief second.

"As well as to be expected," he murmured. He didn't want to think of the fear that had been on her face, or the way her lips had trembled. Ash couldn't be prouder of her. She'd held in her emotions and showed her true strength.

Ash focused his attention back to the screen and paused. Clicking on the picture that caught his eye, he zoomed in on the face.

Bingo.

The big stocky guy.

"He held the gun on me," Ash announced quietly.

Dec, Mac, Brodie, and Myles crowded around Ash to look at the screen.

"Ramello Price." Declan wrote the name down on a piece of paper. According to the file, the large man was muscle for the gang. He had a long list charges including assault, theft, kidnapping, and possession of illegal weapons. The list went on.

Ash stared at the picture, remembering the feel of the gun being pushed into his back.

"Keep going." Mac tapped his chair, breaking through his thoughts.

Ash cleared his throat and clicked onto the next page. He scanned the screen and slowed down on the next familiar face.

Ponytail.

"Him." He clicked on the picture, and it zoomed in the on the man. His thin, stringy hair was lying on his shoulders, but it was definitely the third man who'd been in the alley.

Nate McLean.

Declan scribbled a few notes down on the thug.

Ash continued on, determined he would find the cousin of good old Gus.

Arriving at the last page, he grew anxious. There were hundreds of known associates of the gang. He finally saw the familiar tattooed face staring back at him.

Tattoo Face.

Jamaal Dickerson.

His rap sheet was longer than Ramello's and Nate's combined.

"Here's the last one," he stated.

"I'll send this over to Cameron. He'll get us the information we need," Declan said, closing his notebook.

"How soon will it take?" Mac asked, leaning back against the wall.

Zain and Iker returned with mugs in their hands.

"It shouldn't be too hard for him to come up with something for us. We should be able to move on them tonight," Declan revealed. He was typing on his phone before looking around the room. "Just sent Cameron the names of the three. Should hear back from him ASAP."

"We're going to take them down one by one," Mac began.

Everyone fell silent as they listened to their leader. Ash sat back in his chair, anticipation building. He didn't care what he would have to do to ensure he was prepared for the field, but he'd do it. "I want the Demon Lords to feel us breathing down their necks."

Murmurs of agreement went around. Ash knew without asking, the men here were in this to the end.

When Sarena had been kidnapped by the gang, Ash along with every man on their team had geared up, ready for war to get their sergeant's woman back. They had infiltrated a human trafficking operation with guns blazing to rescue Sarena.

When Declan had needed assistance transporting

Aspen to the airport, they had entered into a fully fledged gun war with her gangster godfather's men.

Now the target was on Ashton.

"Ash, this is too much," Deana exclaimed. She turned to him with a pout.

It was early, and he was escorting her to work. The parking lot had a few cars in it, and the kids had yet to begin to arrive.

"I don't trust any of those men, certainly not Gus and his cousin. Until we've got them off the street, you are going to be under watch." Ash guided his car into an empty spot.

Ash had pulled in a few favors from patrol under the captain's radar. Some of the guys and women would swing by the school a few times a day each day. Deana had put her foot down about a cop in the building, citing the school's security was enough.

"I'll be fine. I hope you are putting forth as much effort to keep yourself safe as you are doing for me," she huffed.

He tossed her a grin and grabbed her hand, tugging her close.

"I can take care of myself," he murmured before covering her lips with his.

Her hand came to rest along his jaw. She pulled back and pressed a chaste kiss to his lips.

"Promise me you will be careful," she whispered.

Her eyes showed her concern, and a smidge of fear crept into her face.

"I promise, Deana," he replied. He covered her hand with his and gave her his killer-watt smile. "Running straight into danger is what I do."

He barked a laugh at her exasperated look. She grabbed her bag and purse reached for the door handle.

"Ash, I'm serious," she said, opening the door and stepping of the vehicle.

Ash's smile disappeared. He released a curse and flew out his door and rushed around the car. He met her as she was tossing her purse over her shoulder.

"Look, Deana." He gripped her shoulders and turned her to him. He stared down into her eyes and wanted to make sure she knew he was serious. "I may be joking about my job, but I'm serious. I'm used to this—"

"Yes, you were used to it when it was just you and you wouldn't have to worry about someone waiting at home scared out of their mind that something would happen to you." Her eyes filled with large tears, and his heart felt as if someone had stabbed him in it.

Shit.

He brought her close, wrapping his arms around her.

He hadn't thought of the repercussions of him joking about the dangerous side of his job. She was right. He also hadn't thought how she would feel when he went out on calls.

That was one thing.

The entire department was behind them when they were sent out on missions.

But doing an operation on side for revenge—that was different.

The stakes were much higher.

And they wouldn't have the backup of the department.

"I'm so sorry, baby. I didn't think," he murmured against her head.

She gripped his shirt tight and leaned her head on his chest. Time seemed to stand still.

Ash was okay with that.

He'd hold Deana forever if he had to.

She pulled back and gazed up at him with the fat tears teetering on the edge of her eyelids. The look on her face practically drove Ash to his knees.

"Just whatever you do, promise me you will come back to me. Whole. No more injuries," she whispered, resting her hand on his chest.

"I'll always come back to you, Deana," he replied.

His throat went raw. He swallowed a few times and met her gaze.

The tears spilled over and slid down her flawless brown skin. He reached up and slowly swiped the wetness from her face.

Nothing else existed around them.

Not the school, not the cars passing by on the street—it was just the two of them.

Ash didn't care that their relationship had gone from zero to sixty in a short matter of time.

Love had hit him square in the chest, and he wasn't going to let it go. He had a good woman standing before him, emotional at the thought of him not returning.

This was all the more reason he needed to end this with the Demon Lords.

To provide a safe city for his woman and kids to grow up in.

Ash's breath caught in his chest at the thought of Deana growing round with his child.

It was a fantasy he certainly wanted to become reality.

"Ash..." She paused, leaning into him.

He welcomed the weight of her. His ribs ached slightly, but he ignored it.

A small smile played on her lips. "I'm falling for you."

"And I you," Ash replied without hesitation.

Her eyes widened at his admission. He lowered his head and kissed her. Her soft lips parted and welcomed him.

The sound of a car pulling into the parking lot had them drawing apart.

Ash's heart raced while he stared into Deana's eyes.

No words were needed.

He knew.

"Hey, lovebirds!" a familiar voice called out.

He turned.

Erin headed their way. "Ain't it a little early for make-out sessions?"

"Morning." Deana greeted her friend with a wave.

"Hey, Erin." Ash smiled and gave her a nod while easing Deana to his side.

"I have to go," Deana announced with a wistful smile.

"I guess I can go let you educate our future generation," he teased.

She stood on tiptoes and pressed a hard kiss to his mouth.

"See you later," she murmured, turning serious again.

His gaze swept her face and memorized every inch it. He was a goner. Head over heels for her.

"I meant what I said." She backed away and hoisted her bag up on her shoulder.

"Yup, got it." He brushed another kiss to her lips before backing away. If he didn't move now, he wouldn't be responsible for his actions. He ran to the driver's side of his vehicle and opened the door. "Get the bad guys, don't get hurt, and come back to you."

18

Get the bad guys, don't get hurt, and come back to you.

Ash's words echoed in Deana's head.

Damn, I love that man.

She hated to get that heavy early in the morning, but it weighed on her heart. She wanted to make sure Ash understood her feelings about him.

A smile came to her lips at the memory of him throwing a wink at her with his good eye before climbing into his car.

Her core clenched at the thought.

He dripped pure sexiness, and she was one lucky lady.

Her classroom was empty at the moment. It was rare she got a full planning period where she didn't have to have at least one or two students she needed to give a little extra help to.

Grabbing her phone from her desk, she brought up

Sarena's number. When they'd met, she and Aspen had given her their numbers.

She created a group text and sent off a message to the both of them.

I caved and became weak. I told him I was worried when he goes out.

She blew out a deep breath. Sarena and Aspen had both encouraged her to be strong for him, but in the moment, she'd broken down and basically cried that he was leaving her to go off and do his job.

Aspen responded first: *First of all, you're not weak.*

Sarena replied: *It will be okay. Ash can handle it.*

Deana was thankful for meeting the two of them. She didn't know how she would ever deal with her anxieties of being the girlfriend of a SWAT officer.

Girlfriend?

A giggle erupted from her lips.

After their exchange this morning, there was no doubt that Ash was her man and she his woman.

She quickly typed out another message: *Thanks, ladies. Something's about to go down, and he's being tight-lipped on what the guys are doing.*

Sarena: *Hmmm...I figured something was going on. Marcas was a little...umm...rambunctious this morning before he left, lol.*

Sarena's response made Deana laugh out loud.

Aspen: *Yeah, Declan was acting weird before he left.*

Sarena made an offer she couldn't refuse: *Happy hour after work tomorrow? Sounds like while the men are off doing their manly thing, we should get together.*

Deana was grateful for the suggestion. She didn't think she wanted to go home to an empty house and sit and wait for Ash to return.

I so need happy hour.

Deana was quick to answer. They made plans to meet at a popular restaurant that wasn't too far from the school the next day. Tossing her phone back in her desk, she felt a bit better knowing she had a support group. A night out with just the girls would be therapy.

"Miss Dawson?" a voice came through the overhead speaker.

"Yes, Mrs. Thomas?" she replied to the school secretary. She stood from her desk and grabbed the assignments the kids would need to work on next for their lesson when they returned.

"There was a letter delivered here to you. I'm sending one of the kids to you with it."

"Okay, thanks!" She began passing the papers out onto the kids' desks. She finished just as the kids shuffled back into the room. "Please hurry to your seats," she instructed.

The kids moaned and groaned seeing the papers on their desks.

She bit back a smile at their faces.

Playtime was over.

"Aw, Miss Dawson." Chip sighed, sitting in his chair. "We were hoping for game time."

Deana chuckled at the misery on his face. She had created a new game to play with the kids for math that they loved. But now wasn't math time, it was time for their reading lesson.

"I'm sorry, Chip, but it's reading time. Let's all get settled, and we'll read the first passage together, and then there are questions that need to be answered."

A collective groan went up in the air.

Deana walked around, calling on random kids to read aloud.

She absolutely loved teaching. Being able to mold the minds of her students gave her purpose in life. Her students became enraptured in the tale they were reading, pausing to raise their hands to ask questions and even start a little discussion amongst them.

A knock sounded at the door. Deana glanced over, having completely forgotten Mrs. Thomas was going to send someone down with the mail. A cute little girl with dark pigtails stood in the doorway.

"Thank you," she said, strolling over to the door.

"You're welcome." The young girl smiled a toothless grin. She handed Deana the envelope before scampering away.

"Okay, class. We did a great job reading and discussing the story. Now I want you to quietly answer the questions. Remember, you can go back to the passage and find the answers," Deana instructed.

Silence fell upon the room. She looked around and could almost hear the wheels of the children's minds spinning.

Walking over to her desk, she stared at the envelope. There was a business logo as the return address, but she didn't remember signing up for anything from them.

Curious, she opened it and found a folded piece of paper. She pulled it loose and opened the sheet.

She bit back a gasp at the message.

Ashes to ashes.

It was typed out in large Arial font. Deana tried to beat down the panic that filled her chest.

Oh God! She sent up a quick prayer that Ash and the guys would be okay.

"Are you all right, Miss Dawson?" a quiet voice asked.

Deana flickered her gaze up to the student who had spoken and found all eyes on her. She quickly recovered and put on a smile.

"Yes." She swallowed hard and refolded the piece of paper. "Yes, everything is just fine."

By the looks on their faces, none of them bought the lie she had just spoken.

These kids are too smart for their own good.

She opened the drawer where her purse was and stashed the letter in it.

She would have to let Ash know about it.

There was no way she could hide this from him.

He was doing just as he had bragged.

Running directly into the face of danger.

Ash's gaze was locked on the car they were tailing. It pulled over and parked along the curb.

"Bingo," Ash murmured, gaze landing on their target stepping from his car. Ash pointed to an empty space a block away. "Park over there."

Gus strolled down the street as if he owned the fucking block.

He would be the first one they'd take down.

He walked toward the corner where a group of young thugs stood.

"That didn't take long at all." Myles chuckled from the driver's seat.

They had received the information from the Gang

Unit immediately. SWAT would take down each of the men, sending a message to the gang that they were not to be messed with.

It gave Ash some satisfaction to know the man's mouth was wired shut from their bar brawl. He curled his hand into a fist. The urge to slam it into Gus's face again was strong.

"Should we call it in now?" Myles asked, holding his cell phone up.

Silence fell upon the car as they observed the men speaking.

"Yeah, I'm sure what they are doing is not illegal." Ash smirked. He had called in a few favors with patrol.

Myles placed the call.

Before their eyes, they watched Gus exchange something with a few of the men.

A drug deal.

Ash chuckled seeing two patrol cars drive up to the corner with their lights on.

The blue-and-red lights had never appeared so good.

"Well, look at that." Myles sarcasm wasn't lost on Ash.

They glanced at each other and shared a fist bump.

Four patrolmen exited their vehicles and strolled up to the men on the corner. They drew their weapons on the men who cooperated with their orders.

Ash almost wished Gus would try to make a run for it.

He'd have an excuse to chase him down.

Ash watched with a grin on his lips. The patrolmen ordered the men to their knees and began searching them.

Including Gus.

Ash remembered the words in the letter that had been thrown through the window of his home.

"Let's roll past and see if our brothers need any help," Ash suggested.

He wanted to ride by so Gus would know it was him.

"I like the way you think." Myles grinned. He threw the car in drive and slowly pulled out into the street, driving up to the scene. Within in minutes, the little stretch of corner was swarming with cops.

They must have found something on each of the men.

Myles braked, allowing Ash to roll his window down. His gaze met Gus's.

Ash smiled and aimed his gun-shaped fingers at Gus.

Bang, bang, he mouthed.

Gus's eyes grew wide once he realized it was Ash in the car.

Their laughter grew watching the men be handcuffed and read their Miranda rights.

Myles pulled off into the light traffic. Ash felt a small twinge of satisfaction with Gus being arrested. He had quite the rap, and the Gang Unit had a solid case they were bringing up on him. He wouldn't be getting out of jail any time soon.

"One down," he murmured, sitting back in his chair.

"And an entire organization to take down," Myles replied, glancing over at him. "You don't look too happy. I thought you'd be ecstatic that the asshole who got you jumped was arrested."

Ash shook his head. "He's a little fish in a big sea. I've been thinking. This thing between Deana and me is getting serious quick. What happens next time if someone comes after her? I don't care if they come for me. I can take care of myself, but if anything were—"

"It won't," Myles sharp response cut Ash off. "You know the guys are going to ensure our families remain safe."

Ash looked at his friend and met his gaze before Myles turned his attention back to the road.

"Thanks, man," he mumbled, running a hand along his face.

"And let them try to come for us." Myles snickered.

The sound sent a chill down Ash's spine. Myles

was one man Ash wouldn't want to be on his bad side. "We're the baddest muthafuckers with a badge."

"You damn right we are," Ash agreed with a grin spreading. Of course, Myles would bring him out of his funk and make him feel better.

The Demon Lords wouldn't know what hit them.

SWAT was about to go hunting.

19

"Just breathe," Erin advised, pulling her car into the parking lot of Ash's precinct. She shut off the engine and turned to face Deana.

After school, Deana had rushed over to Erin's classroom and showed her the letter she had received.

"We're going to march in there, and you are going to demand to see your man so you can show him the note."

Deana stared at her friend without saying a word before nodding.

Erin was right.

Ash had to know.

This couldn't be anything else but a threat against him. He would need to know about it so that he could protect himself. Deana wouldn't be able to live with herself if something happened to him.

"Of course I'm going to tell him. Thanks for coming with me," she said, reaching for Erin's hand.

"What are friends for?" Erin laughed, squeezing Deana's hand. "Let's go."

They exited the vehicle and walked into the brick building. Deana didn't know if Ash was there or not, but she had to get to him.

Entering the lobby, they were met by a weathered, older-looking woman who Deana instantly knew didn't take any shit from anyone.

"Can I help you?" The woman pushed her glasses on top of her graying hair. Even though the words spilled from her mouth, she didn't appear as if she truly cared about why Deana and Erin were coming to the police station.

The bustle of cops and detectives behind her caught Deana's eye. No sign of anyone she knew from Ash's team.

"Um, hi." Deana swallowed hard and moved up to the counter. "My name is Deana Dawson, and I need to see Officer Ashton Fraser."

The woman eyed her up and down and smirked.

"What do you need with him?" She leaned her hip against the counter and adjusted her glasses on her head.

"I just need to speak with him. It's regarding something he's working on," Deana replied. She felt a presence come to her side and knew it was Erin.

"I'm not sure he's here. I can get one of the other officers to help you—"

"No, it has to be Officer Fraser or maybe Myles or Mac?" Deana was quick to cut her off.

There was no way she would share what was on the piece of paper in her purse with anyone but a member of Ash's SWAT team if he was unavailable. She couldn't wait for him to get home because there was no telling if he was out in the streets tracking a member of the gang down.

If Ash wasn't available, SWAT only.

"I see." The woman paused with her hand on the telephone beside her. Her eyes flickered between Erin and Deana before turning away. "Hey, Reeves! Get over here." She flagged down a passing officer in uniform.

"Hey, Karla. What's up?" The officer walked over to her. His face was young-looking and clean-cut. His gaze paused on Deana and Erin before going back to Karla's.

"These two are here to see Fraser, but I think he's out. Can you take her back to SWAT and see who's there? She only wants one of them." Karla sighed.

"Sure." Surprise registered on his face. He waved them around the counter.

"Thank you," Deana said to Karla. She tried to give

her a smile, but the lady grumbled and turned her back. Deana wasn't sure what she said, but she was sure it was something about SWAT and groupies.

"Hello, ladies, I'm Officer Reeves," he introduced himself with his hand outstretched.

"I'm Deana, and this is my friend, Erin." Deana reached forward and took his hand in a firm shake.

"Hello," Erin greeted him, taking his hand in a shake, too.

"I can escort you back to the SWAT guys. Come with me." He motioned for them to follow him.

Deana walked behind the officer and observed the busy station. They strolled past what she assumed was the bull pen where there was an area with a sea of desks and personnel.

"If Ash isn't here, what are you going to do? Call him?" Erin asked.

"I tried to call him, but he didn't answer," Deana murmured. She'd had to beat down her nervousness when his voicemail had come on earlier. She hadn't left a voicemail, not knowing what to say.

"How do you know Fraser?" Reeves asked, glancing back over his shoulder, obviously having heard Erin's question.

"I'm his girlfriend," she replied. She had to fight to keep a smile from spreading.

Erin shoved her with her elbow, and Deana stumbled a bit. She lost the battle, her lips curving up in the corners.

"Oh, nice." They were now away from the main bustle of the precinct and were in a quieter area lined with offices. There were a few people who walked past with curious looks. "Have a seat here, and I'll see which of the guys are here to help you."

"Thank you," she said. Deana hefted her purse up on her shoulder and watched him walk away.

"Did he give you the creeps?" Erin muttered, standing by her.

"Erin!" Deana chuckled, shaking her head at her friend.

"I'm just saying. He's just weird." Erin shrugged and moved over to the window near a row of chairs.

"You watch too many cop shows." Deana ambled over and joined her. The window revealed the back of the precinct and a parking lot for employees.

"He looks like the type of guy who gets a kick out of handing out tickets." Erin snickered.

Deana rolled her eyes, watching a few cars drive by the window.

"Deana?"

She turned around and found Ash and Myles standing there with Officer Reeves behind them.

"Ash!" She rushed forward, unable to contain herself.

His arms immediately opened, and he caught her with a grunt. Her heart raced.

He was okay.

"What's wrong, babe?" he asked, laying a kiss on the top of her head.

She pulled back and found curiosity lining his face.

"I was scared," she began but caught herself seeing Officer Reeves standing near Myles.

Ash followed her gaze.

"I got it, Reeves. Thanks." He nodded to Reeves, dismissing him.

"Anytime. Let me know if you need anything," Officer Reeves offered before swiveling on his heel and heading toward the direction they had come from.

"Here, let's go somewhere private to talk," Myles offered, motioning to a door. He must have sensed something was wrong.

Ash put his arm around her shoulders and guided her into the room. He flicked the light on, and she was met with what looked like the briefing rooms they showcased on those television shows Erin loved to watch.

Myles closed the door behind them. Erin took a seat at the table in the front.

"What's wrong?" Ash repeated, turning her to him.

Deana dug around in her purse and drew the envelope out. She opened it and handed it to Ash.

"This was delivered to me at work today."

He took it from her and glanced over at Myles first before focusing on the letter. He pulled it out of the envelope and scanned the sheet of paper. Deana watched his gaze narrow on it, and his face hardened ever so slightly. She bit her lip and knew he was masking his emotions from her.

He handed it to Myles who took one look at it and stalked out of the room.

"I'm going to handle this," Ash vowed, resting his hands on her shoulders. "We have a plan."

"Ash, this is getting out of hand. These men are no joke," she stated. A rush of feelings was overtaking her that she couldn't explain.

"I think you need to listen to her," Erin chimed in from her seat.

Ash nodded and brought Deana into the circle of his arms. The feel of him surrounding her calmed her down.

The door opened, and a parade of men entered.

Ash's team.

She had quickly forgotten how big they were, but them decked out in all black with the SWAT logo brandished on their chests and weapons lining their bodies took her breath away.

Sweet Mary and Joseph.
What was she worried for again?

There was fear on Deana's face, and Ash detested it. It had taken everything he had to rein in his anger at the short note.

Ashes to ashes.

How dare they involve Deana. How dare they instill fear into her.

The Demon Lords would pay.

"This was delivered to the school or to your home?" Mac's voice cut through the room.

"The school," Deana answered, pulling away slightly.

Ash kept his arm around her, not wanting to let her go.

He and Myles had just returned from their little joyride when Reeves had caught him. The guy had been coming around more and more now that he knew the trials for SWAT was coming up. Ash had tried to brush past him and ignore him until he'd said a pretty little woman claiming to be his girlfriend was at the precinct looking for him.

"Who dropped it off? Did it go through the postal service?" Declan asked.

"I don't know," Deana replied.

Ash rubbed her shoulder, offering her support.

"I got a call from the school's secretary saying I had a letter delivered."

"Look at the return address," Myles said, handing the envelope to Declan.

"Dolly's Bakery," Declan murmured. He turned his attention to Deana. "Have you ever shopped there before?"

Deana shook her head.

"Brodie, go run a check on this bakery. See if there is any connection with the Demon Lords," Mac ordered.

Dec handed the envelope off to Brodie.

"Be right back." Brodie gave a nod and stepped from the room.

"Ash, you take the girls home—" Mac began, but Ash shook his head.

"There is no way I'm sitting out on this one." Ash already knew where Mac was headed. His ribs would be fine. He'd wrap them up and be good as new. As long as there was breath in his lungs, he could shoot a gun.

Tonight, they had planned to raid a crack house where it was a common hangout spot for Nate and Ramello. This raid would knock out two birds with one stone.

"You sure you're good?" Zain asked, cocking an eyebrow.

"Ash, why don't you sit this one out?" Deana turned her large brown eyes on him.

His heart stuttered, and he almost caved.

He had to go with his team.

The door swung open, and Ash froze.

Captain Spook.

"What the hell is going on in here?" Captain Spook demanded. His gaze swept the room, and Ash could have sworn the temperature dropped a few degrees.

No one said a word.

"I'm sorry, sir," Deana began.

Ash's eyes widened as he turned to look at her.

"The guys are in here because of me."

"Who are you?" Spook asked, focusing his attention on Deana.

"I'm Deana Dawson. Ash's girlfriend." She stepped forward and offered her hand.

The captain, a true gentlemen, shook her hand.

"And this is my friend, Erin."

"So please tell me, Miss Dawson. Why would my SWAT team be gathering together because of you?"

Deana glanced at him, and Ash gave her a slight shake of his head, but she must not have caught it.

This was the last thing they needed.

The captain would have all their asses.

This was it. They'd be busted down to meter maids or something else low.

"I received a letter delivered to my job that was a threat to Ash." She rested a hand on his arm, and he couldn't be mad at her. She was trying to protect him.

"Did you now." Spook's gaze landed on Ash who held his gaze without blinking.

It was time to let the captain in on what was going on.

"And why would my officer be sent threatening letters?" Spook crossed his arms in front of his chest.

Ash glanced at Mac who nodded to him. He met each of his teammates' gazes and knew without a doubt they were all in this together. If they got bumped down to traffic, well, they'd be the best damn traffic team in Columbia.

"I'm sure you heard about Ash in the fight at the bar. Well, come to find out the guy he fought is a cousin of that gang...what's the name again?" She turned her big brown eyes to Ash, and his heart melted.

"Demon Lords," he muttered.

Captain's face didn't budge. It was as if it were made of stone while Deana went into details about the gang and getting the letter.

She finished telling her story, and the room fell silent.

Ash was thankful she was unaware of certain

details. He focused his attention on the captain whose hard stare was locked on him.

"Fraser. Mac. My office," the captain barked. He strode to the door and pulled it open. He turned and glared at them. "Now."

20

The door slammed behind Captain Spook. There was no doubt he was pissed. Ash stood next to Mac in solid formation waiting to get their asses handed to them. Ash stared off at the far wall with his hands collapsed behind his back.

"Why am I not surprised? I should strip you of your damn badges for this shit," Spook muttered, walking to stand in front of his desk. His scowl was deep. "Was your woman speaking truth, Fraser?"

Ash's gaze met the captain's. He gave a nod. "Yes, sir."

"And you all decided that you would handle it on your own?" The captain leaned back against his desk. He was one hard son of a bitch, and Ash only hoped he made it out the office with the skin on his back. "On whose orders?"

"Mine, sir," Mac replied, taking a step forward. Of course Mac would take responsibility for the entire team. He was their leader, and not once had he hesitated to jump into the mess with Ash.

"Is that right?" Spook cocked an eyebrow. His gaze flickered between Ash and Mac.

"We bleed blue blood, sir. When one of our own is under attack, it's our job to win the fucking war." Mac turned his hard eyes to Ash.

Ash gave him a solid nod, feeling the love from his team. Mac's words hit him deep in his gut.

These were his brothers, and they would be right by his side just as he would be by theirs.

"You got that fucking right." The captain sighed, standing straight up again.

Ash shot his gaze back to his superior in shock.

This wasn't the response he had been expecting.

"Excuse me?" Ash asked, unsure he'd heard the captain clearly.

"It's an honorable thing. I respect how deep your bond is with each other. I wish all units were the same." He ran a hand along his head and narrowed his gaze on them. "You're going after the Demon Lords?"

"Yes, sir," Ash and Mac answered simultaneously, without hesitation.

The gang would pay.

It was time the do a clean sweep of the streets to make it safe for the good people of Columbia.

"What do you need from me?"

Ash glanced at Mac.

The captain never failed to surprise him.

"We're planning a raid on a drug house tonight. It's a known hangout of a couple of the men we are targeting. We need official orders," Mac said, folding his arms in front of his chest.

"Consider it done. What other departments are involved?"

What they had planned to do would have been off the books. Now, with the support of their captain, they could pull out the full arsenal.

"Gang Unit. They've been helping us," Ash admitted.

Spook nodded before walking around his desk.

"Get the hell out of here and do what you do best. I expect reports on my desk first thing in the morning," Spook said, sitting in his chair. "Next time there's a problem, I expect to be notified immediately."

"Yes, sir," Ash and Mac answered together.

Ash turned on his heel with Mac behind him. They exited the office and didn't look back. Rounding the corner, Ash finally breathed a sigh of relief and paused.

He faced Mac who stood next to him.

"Did you think we were going to get knocked down to parking duties?" Ash asked, lips curving up in the corner. Relief filled him knowing the captain fully supported them.

"Fuck, I was thinking mall security," Mac muttered.

Ash chuckled, running a hand through his hair.

"Shit." Ash shook his head, cringing at the thought.

The muffled sound of a phone ringing interrupted them. Mac and Ash both reached for their phones, but it was Mac's that was ringing.

"Mac," he barked into it.

Ash stood beside him and glanced down at his. They had a few hours until they were to meet up with the Gang Unit.

"How the fuck you get this number?" Mac growled.

Ash's attention immediately cut to Mac.

Who the hell was he speaking to?

Mac put the phone on speaker.

"Don't worry about how I got your number," a smooth voice said. "Just know that you are the one who I need to speak to. Since it was your men who took out the previous head of the Demon Lords, I felt it was only right I call you and let you know there is a new leader now."

"Is that right?" Ash said, sliding his phone into his cargo pants pocket. He didn't like where this call was going. "And who are we speaking to?"

"Is that Officer Ashton Fraser?" The person chuckled. "I'm glad I caught you both at the same time so I don't have to repeat myself."

"I'm going to hang up if you don't get to the fucking point," Mac snapped.

"So impatient, but that's okay, I'm going to teach you patience. Silas was an idiot. He loved cat-and-mouse games, but I'm not like that. I'm a direct and to-the-point type of man."

"You have two seconds." Patience was not one of Mac's virtues.

"You did us a favor taking Silas out. Give my regards to Sergeant Owen for having such a fantastic aim. This will be your only warning from me. The Demon Lords will prevail, and if you don't move out my way, you will get run the fuck over."

The line went dead.

Deana sat in the car, worried. Ash had yet to say a word to her.

"Ash, you have to tell me. Did I do wrong in coming to the station?" she asked.

"What?" He glanced at her and shook his head. "No, babe. You did right in coming to me with what you received. Something else came up."

"Okay." She sat back and stared out the window. She wasn't convinced that he wasn't upset with her. Ash would have to understand that she was concerned for him and wanted him safe.

He pulled into her driveway and shut off the car. Deana sat still, watching him exit the vehicle and march around to her door. She took his hand and allowed him to assist her out. He entwined their hands and walked her up the stairs.

Once inside, she shut the door behind them and turned to Ash.

His jaw was set in a hard line.

He was pissed.

"I'm sorry," she breathed, her shoulders slumped. She didn't want him mad at her.

He ran a hand along his face and shook his head. He stepped to her and rested his hands on the door beside her head, trapping her.

"I'm not mad at you. I promise," he said, staring into her eyes. "I've just got a lot on my mind and I don't want anything to happen to you."

"Me? They are threatening you!" she scoffed.

A smile broke out on his lips, and his face relaxed.

There he was.

The man she'd fallen in love with.

She paused and relished the realization of what she'd just thought.

Yes, I love this man.

Without a doubt, Ashton Fraser had buried himself in her heart.

"And what is my little schoolteacher going to do? Take her red pen and grade the bad guys' performance?" He chuckled.

Deana smiled, shaking her head at his bad joke.

"I'll do anything to protect my man," she murmured, turning serious. She leaned against him, dropping her purse so she could wrap her arms around his waist.

"Is that so?" His smile faded as he bent down and pressed his lips to hers. It was a quick kiss and certainly not enough.

Deana wanted—no, needed—more.

She knew he and his SWAT team had something dangerous in mind. There was no telling what he'd been up to before she'd arrived at the station.

She pushed Ash backwards until he was against the wall. She slid her hands down his toned waist and reached for his jeans. She undid the button and pushed the zipper down.

Deana tore her mouth from Ash and promptly knelt before him on the floor.

You love them hard and good every day as if it's their last.

"Deana," he gasped.

His strangled voice coaxed her on. This was something she had to do. She needed to have every ounce of her man before sending him off to the dangers of his job.

She made quick work of pushing his jeans down to his ankles and hooked her fingers along his boxer briefs, pulling them down slowly. His cock sprang free, capturing her attention.

She reached for him, encircling his length with her hand and slid it along the smooth shaft. Ash threaded his fingers into her hair with a grunt.

She licked his entire cock, taking her first taste of him.

Deana guided him to her lips and welcomed the mushroom tip between her lips. She flickered her gaze up to meet his while she eased more of him into her mouth.

A string of curses escaped him.

His grip in her hair tightened.

He slowly thrust his hips forward, sending his cock farther into her mouth. She sucked hard while pumping her hand along him. The taste of him was divine, and she never wanted to stop.

"Deana," he whispered, tugging on her hair.

She ignored him and kept going. She closed her eyes and basked in pleasing Ash.

She wanted to show him how much she cared for him.

How much she needed him.

And what he had to return to.

His muscles tensed, and she opened her eyes, meeting his.

He pulled her off his cock.

"Hey!" she protested.

He snatched her up from the floor and pushed her against the wall.

"I wasn't done."

"For now you are," he muttered. His hands quickly peeled her clothes off. He lifted her up by the back of her knees. Her legs automatically wrapped around him. "You're going to be the death of me."

He lined up the blunt tip of his cock and thrust forward with a shout.

"Ash!" she cried out. She dug her nails into his shoulders while hanging on for the ride.

"This is going to be fast and hard, pretty lady." His lips brushed against her ear as he tucked his face into the crook of her neck.

His cock went deep inside her with each thrust. Their cries of passion were the only sounds echoing in the house.

"Yes," she hissed.

His hands dug into her thighs while holding her in place.

She parted her lips, and soon his were there covering them. His tongue thrust deep inside her mouth. Ash was consuming her, and Deana loved every moment of it.

She squeezed her legs tighter while he hammered his cock home.

She broke their kiss, a cry erupting from her lips. Her orgasm was rushing toward her, and there was nothing she could do to stop it. Her body trembled with the need to release.

"Ash," she chanted over and over. Her walls clamped down on him, and a scream erupted from her. A hard orgasm washed over her, blinding her to nothing but the feeling of Ashton deep inside her.

He pumped a few more times before his orgasm took him. His hips paused while he let out a strangled cry, filling her with his release. A warmth spread through her, and she accepted every ounce of him.

Deana wrapped her arms around his neck tight, not ready to let him go.

She was quickly learning that the hardest part of loving a SWAT officer was letting him run off into danger.

Tears blurred her vision. She squeezed her eyes shut, not wanting him to see them.

She'd be strong for Ash.

He would need her.

"I didn't hurt you, did I?" he murmured against her shoulder.

"I should be asking you that." She chuckled, blinked away the tears, and held him close to her.

"I'm a big boy," he joked.

Don't I know it, she thought, squeezing her muscles around his semi-soft cock.

He wasn't lying either. His cock stretched and filled her perfectly.

"Then let's go to the bedroom, big boy." A sassy grin spread. If he was leaving her to go do what he and his team did best, then she would certainly send him off right.

"Yes, ma'am. I like the way you think."

21

It had been too long since Ash had donned his ballistics vest. He wasn't meant to spend his time behind the desk. Out in the field with a gun in his hand was where he belonged.

Leaving Deana's bed had been one of the hardest things he'd had to do. Her warm, supple thighs called to him. He had spent as much time as he could in between them. The feeling of her gripping his cock, the sound of her cries all stuck with him on the drive to the station.

Dressed in his black fatigues, vest, and his body lined with weapons was a homecoming for Ash.

Tonight's operation would be no different from any other drug raid. Only this time, Ash had a score to settle with two of the men.

"ETA is five minutes," Zain announced.

The air in the BEAR was tense. Each man was obviously mentally preparing for the mission.

With the captain's support, they officially had the precinct backing them up along with the gang division.

Ash's gaze met that of Myles who gave him a slight nod. His longtime friend was decked out just as Ash was.

"We'll get them," Myles said, apparently knowing what Ash was thinking.

The gangsters thought they'd scare Ash. They hadn't faced him man-to-man but had to jump him like the cowards they were.

His bruising had almost faded from his skin, and his ribs barely caused a twinge of pain.

"You're damn right we'll get the sons of bitches." Brodie smirked, placing his helmet on top of his head. "We'll get to show them how Columbia's finest gets down."

Ash nodded to each of his brothers in blue.

Only tonight, they were brothers in black.

"There's a new leader to the Demon Lords," Mac began, gaining the attention of every man in the vehicle. "His name is Victor Huff, also known as House. I sent you his rap sheet and I hope you all had the chance to look it over."

Ash nodded. Huff had a rap sheet that would make most of the infamous mobsters in history look like choir boys. He had been involved in everything from running drugs from Mexico, to human trafficking, to racketeering, and he'd even beat a murder case or three. It was also rumored he'd killed his own father.

The man was bad news, and he would be someone they'd have to keep an eye on until they could get him off the streets, too.

"Tonight, we're going to seize whatever we find. From our intel, there should be a hefty amount of drugs in this house," Declan chimed in.

"You would have thought they'd learned the last time we hit them up." Iker shook his head.

"They're greedy. They've been shipping their supply to Atlanta and Miami, and I'm sure they're making a killing." Ash sat back in his seat.

Columbia was a prime location for the big drug dealers. With the drug epidemic, business was booming, and with them about to cut into their supply, the Demon Lords would feel it.

"We're here," Mac barked, standing from his seat as the truck took a corner.

Ash blew out a deep breath and tried not to think of anything but the operation at hand.

He'd been on countless raids as a SWAT member. This was not new for him. It was like riding a bike. Even though he'd missed a few jobs with the guys, he hadn't forgotten his training.

This job, they'd pour out of the truck in a direct formation and head straight toward the crack house.

They wouldn't give anyone a chance to scramble.

They were taking the house by storm.

Ash pulled his mask up to hide his face and ensured his helmet was on properly. He grabbed his MP5 and stood.

Tension was mounting.

This was what they did.

Go round up the bad buys.

"SWAT." Mac stood before the door and turned to look at them. His hard gaze met the eye of every man in the BEAR. The air grew still as they knew what Mac was about to say. The vehicle drew to a halt. "It's time to hunt."

He pushed open the door of the truck, and they filed out swiftly. The street was dark and empty.

SWAT would be the ones invading the structure and ensuring that it was safe. They'd be responsible for taking down and eliminating all threats so that the uniforms could come into the building.

The full moon was high, providing them plenty of light to see.

Ash raised his weapon and aimed it while running behind Declan. They had practiced this drill countless amount of times until they could practically do it in their sleep.

The house sat on the end of a run-down street. Most of the houses were boarded up and abandoned.

The mistake the gang had made was the high electric bill had set off a warning with the electric company. The cops were able to confirm the house was being used to prepare drugs in order to hit the streets.

Well, tonight, that wouldn't be happening.

The drugs they would be confiscating would be destroyed.

This would always hit the gang in their pockets, hard.

Want to piss off a gang lord?

Take away their money.

They rushed up the stairs with Brodie in the lead. The windows were covered with brown paper, blocking the view inside. He used his ram, and with two hits, the front door gave way.

They moved in solid formation into the house. Screams echoed through the air.

"CPD! Freeze!" Brodie shouted.

Ash swung his gun around, his gaze sweeping the room. Young women, naked, sat at tables scattered in what should have been the living room, and to the left, the dining room.

One of the tables before them were all the items needed to weigh and measure the white powdery substance to put in little baggies.

"Don't fucking move," Declan shouted to one of the men in the corner.

While Brodie, Declan, and Mac began securing the rooms, Ash, Myles, Zain, and Iker pushed forward through the building. Their sweep had to be swift. Once they had breached the house, their backup and support would surround the property to ensure no one escaped.

They stalked down a short hallway to the kitchen, finding a man at the stove, cooking up what Ash assumed was crack cocaine.

These types of places were known for not only processing the most expensive cocaine, but also crack that could be broken down and injected into junkies' veins.

The cook made a move to the back door.

"Freeze!" Myles growled. "Hands where we can see them."

Iker instantly advanced in on him. They slammed against the door. Iker immediately had the guy's arms behind his back and held in place.

"Is there anyone else in the house?" Ash shouted, training his weapon on the floor while Iker cuffed him.

The criminal just stared at the floor without responding. Men like this wouldn't want to be labeled a snitch.

He sucked his teeth and allowed Iker to turn him and place him a sitting position on the floor.

Well, what do you know.

The cook was Nate McLean—Ponytail.

Ash released a curse and glanced at Myles and Zain. "Up we go."

The three of them headed toward the stairs. Zain led the way with Myles in the middle and Ash bringing up the rear. They rushed up to the second level where it appeared empty.

Coming upon the first room, Zain burst in. Myles and Ash followed.

Ash swung his weapon around, not seeing anyone.

Myles opened the closet. "Clear."

They moved to the next bedroom, clearing it along with closets in the hallways.

Nothing.

Ash's breathing was labored from adrenaline coursing through his veins. It felt damn good to be doing what he loved to do.

He swept the area with his keen gaze, and it landed on the last door.

Ash turned and motioned to Myles and Zain.

According to the plans of the house, there was a basement but no attic. Ash was certain Mac would have the basement searched and secured.

Raising his weapon, he crept forward silently. He held his breath, gripped the handle, and pushed it open.

A small bathroom.

He stepped inside with Myles behind him waiting at the door.

Ash willed his heart to slow down.

Ash kept his weapon trained on the dark curtain and pulled it back.

A figure jumped forward and slammed into Ash's body, knocking his weapon from his hands. The strap caused it to swing behind him.

Ash released a grunt as they fell against the sink.

Curses filled the air.

He grappled with the figure, blocking a blow to the face and landing a good one to the attacker's body.

"CPD," he growled, wrestling to get the body off him. He flipped them around and forced the man against the wall, face-first.

"Freeze, or I will shoot you in the face," Myles hollered from the doorway.

"I ain't did nothing." The guy groaned.

Ash held his forearm against the back of the thug's neck and his body to hold him in place.

"You just attacked an officer of the law. I'd say that was something," Ash bit out, pressing him harder into the wall. He was pissed he'd been taken off guard. Taking out his ties, he secured the man's wrist behind his back.

"Shit. I didn't mean to. I didn't know who you were," he cried out while Ash whipped him around.

A smile formed on Ash's lips.

"Doesn't matter, asshole." Ash chuckled.

Jamaal Dickerson—Gus's cousin.

"I'm serious," Jamaal stressed. "I didn't know."

Ash pulled his face mask off. Jamaal's eyes widened, and a curse spilled from his lips.

"You clear up there?" Mac's voice came through Ash's earpiece.

"Yeah, we're clear. We've got one up here," Ash responded. He yanked Jamaal off the wall and pushed him toward Myles.

Tonight's raid couldn't have ended better.

Ash stalked behind them, watching Myles and Zain guide Jamaal down to the first floor.

Tonight, a message would be sent to House.

Don't fuck with SWAT.

22

Deana pulled into the restaurant's parking lot where she was to meet Sarena and Aspen. She hadn't seen Ash since he'd left her bed last night. All day at work, she'd been worried and barely able to concentrate. What helped her get through the day was receiving a few texts from him here and there.

He'd checked in with her to notify her he was okay.

She didn't care what had happened when he'd left last night.

She just wanted him to come back to her in one piece and with no new bruises.

It had been a trying day at work. State testing was upon them. Her students were worried and stressed. She'd had to fight to stay focused and give her students the attention they needed in order to help them with their exams.

She pulled phone from her purse, swiped the screen, and scrolled through her text messages.

I miss you, babe. Don't drink too much with the girls. I'll meet you at your place tonight.

She smiled. He had been ecstatic that she had befriended Sarena and Aspen. According to Ash, he and the guys hung out away from work, and it would be good for her to get to be friends with their women.

She stashed her phone back in her purse and exited the vehicle. Deana glanced around and took in the crowd of people heading toward the restaurant.

Hoisting her purse strap up on shoulder, she walked toward the building, following the crowd.

Once she was inside, her gaze wandered the atrium.

"Can I help you?" asked a slim, tall blonde dressed in the restaurant's signature uniform of black top and jeans.

"I'm looking for my two friends. I think they're at the bar." Deana stepped over to the podium.

"Go right ahead and look for them, hun." She waved toward the bar area.

"Thanks!" Deana walked past her, and her gaze instantly zoomed in on Sarena and Aspen sitting together. Her lips curled up into a smile as she made her way to them. "Hey, ladies!"

"Deana!" Sarena's grin widened. She stood and instantly opened her arms for a hug.

Deana greeted them both with hugs. She instantly

felt welcomed by the two as if they had been longtime friends.

"Finally! We've just ordered our first drink. What do you want?" Aspen asked with a laugh, waving the bartender over to them. He was average-looking, and his t-shirt fit him snug. Deana was pretty certain that was done on purpose to help ensure he got good tips. Her gaze dropped down to his name tag: Mike.

"I'll take a vodka and cranberry," she requested, sitting on an empty stool.

"Give me one sec, ma'am." Mike tossed her a wink before turning away.

"How are you holding up?" Sarena asked, looking over her glass.

"I'm okay," Deana lied. She gave her best smile but instantly knew neither of the women believed her.

"Here you go. One cranberry and vodka," Mike announced, setting her glass in front of her.

"Thanks." She pulled out a few bills to pay and tip him. She would have to make sure she didn't drink too much. She was driving and didn't want to get too inebriated. Grabbing her glass, she took a healthy sip.

"There's a booth opened up. Let's go snag that." Aspen pointed to an area in the corner.

They hurried over to the empty booth. Aspen surprised Deana with how fast she could move with her slight limp.

"Let's try this again. How are you holding up?" Sarena's perfectly sculpted eyebrow rose high on her forehead.

"All right. The truth." The girls giggled at her dramatic eyeball. "Last night, Ash left, and I know they went on a raid. He's been gone since last night—"

"And did you take heed to my advice?" Sarena asked, resting her chin on her hand.

Deana laughed. Her cheeks warmed, but she already felt a sisterly bond growing between the three of them.

"Yes. I. Did." She snapped her finger and thumb with each word, proud she had been able to do as Sarena had suggested.

Love them hard and good every day as if it's their last.

Ash had fallen asleep in her arms. When she had woken up, he'd been long gone.

"I'm not mad at you." Aspen chuckled. "I just love hearing Dec curse while getting ready for work. I pity whoever they were after."

"Tell me about it." Sarena snorted. "Mac's glare alone is enough make any criminal just throw down their weapon and handcuff themselves."

Deana giggled along with the girls. Just thinking of bad guys surrendering at the sight of Mac was comical.

"Well, I hope your husband uses his glare tonight."

Deana sighed. She just wanted Ash to come home to her in one piece.

A waiter appeared at their table just as they were finishing off their drinks. They placed their order of appetizers they'd decided to share and the second round of drinks.

"How's everything going with you and Ash?" Aspen asked, turning toward Deana.

"Wonderful. He's the sweetest guy I've ever met," Deana replied, trying not to grin too wide. She couldn't help herself. Just thinking about Ash had her heart pounding. "How's the wedding planning coming?" she asked Aspen.

"Great. Declan is more involved than I thought he'd want to be." Aspen shrugged.

"You didn't forget he's used to bossing people around, right?" Sarena scoffed. "Between him and Mac, I don't know who is bossier."

Aspen rolled her eyes. "It's going to be magical. The wedding of my—our— dreams."

"Sounds amazing." Deana smiled. She loved weddings and couldn't wait to be able to plan hers. She'd love something outdoors on the beach. Just sand, friends, and getting married to the man of her dreams.

Ash's face came to mind.

"Here you go." The waiter reappeared. He had a

welcoming grin while delivering their food and drinks. They had ordered enough food to feed an army.

Deana dove into hers after the waiter ensured they had everything they would need.

"We have about two hundred people invited for the wedding," Aspen began. She paused to dig in her purse before turning back to Deana. She slid a pale-pink envelope across the table. "Consider yourself officially invited."

"I'll see ya'll lazy motherfuckers tomorrow," Ash called out with a wave.

"See you, man." Myles held his fist out.

Ash hit it with his, walking past him. He headed out of the locker room and strode toward the back entrance of the precinct.

The day had been long and grueling.

SWAT had been on the hunt.

They'd hit another location owned by the Demon Lords.

This time, they'd done a sweep of a well-known crack house. Eleven men had been arrested in the raid. It felt damn good to clean up the bad neighborhoods.

They had been working on another plan that would draw out the gang leader. Not wanting to let too many people know what they had planned, only SWAT members knew the details.

They would take down this leader, and if another one popped up, then they'd just take them out, too.

They would not stop until they had wiped out the criminal activity in their area.

Exiting the building, Ash strode to his car with his duffle bag in hand. The sun had gone down, and he couldn't wait to get to Deana's side.

It had been torture being away from her. He had planned to head to her house once he got off work. He'd taken his shower in the precinct so he wouldn't smell like guns and sweat.

He hit the unlock button on his key fob, and the sounds of the vehicle unlocking echoed through the quiet air. He paused next to the truck, sensing a something behind him.

Glancing over his shoulder, Ash caught sight of two figures standing there. His muscles grew tense while he turned to face them, dropping his bag on the ground.

"What is this?" Ash snapped. He eyed the men, taking in their physically fit forms. They were obviously the muscle for their employer.

Whatever they wanted or were about to do, Ash wasn't going to go down lightly.

"Consider it a welcoming committee, Officer Frasier," the first one said with a dry chuckle.

"Not interested." Ash balled his hands up into tight fists, ready to defend himself. He may not be able to completely take them both on, but he'd go down swinging.

"You don't get a choice," the second one barked, moving toward Ash. He pulled out a gun from underneath his jacket and aimed it at Ash. "He wants to see you."

"Who wants to see me?" Ash wasn't intimidated by the weapon. They were not too far from the precinct.

Someone would see what was going on.

"Mr. Huff."

Ash narrowed his eyes on them.

Victor Huff. The new boss of the Demon Lords was requesting him.

Ash laughed dryly.

"So I take it your boss isn't too happy right now?" Ash crossed his arms defiantly.

"You're coming with us," the first one stated, ignoring Ash's taunt.

"And we are not asking. We can do this the easy way or the hard way. Your choice." The second one waved the gun from Ash to a dark van parked a few spots away from Ash's truck.

He contemplated his options, and right now, they were limited.

Risk running from them and taking a bullet or go with them and still risk a bullet.

"Well, lead the way, fellas." Ash snorted, sliding his keys into his pocket.

At least if he waited, he could potentially get away unscathed.

Curiosity was burning inside him about meeting the new leader of the gang.

Their recent raid had cost the Demon Lords a pretty penny. It didn't take a genius to know the head of the gang would be pissed.

The first man walked ahead of Ash while the one toting the gun followed behind.

"You guys shouldn't have gone through all the trouble," Ash joked, trying to keep his anger at bay.

Two gangsters, guns, and an unmarked van were not looking good for Ash.

He bit back a curse.

He should have waited for Myles and walked out with him.

With his friend at his side, Ash was sure the two of them could have taken on Goon One and Goon Two together.

The man in front of Ash opened the door to the van and turned to face Ash.

"I hope you got these same lame-ass jokes when you meet with Mr. Huff," he said.

"I'm sure I can think of a few more." Ash sniffed.

He bent down in front of Ash and began sliding his hands swiftly along Ash's pants. He stood upright, reaching into Ash's pocket, pulling out his cell phone. He tossed it on the ground before motioning for Ash to hold his arms out.

"Nice bracelet," he said, resting his hand on Ash's wrist.

"It's mine, asshole." Ash glared at him, snatching his arm away.

Once he was satisfied that Ash didn't have any weapons on his body, he stepped back.

"You should have a little more respect for authority figures," Ash replied, meeting his gaze head-on. He was shoved from behind. "What the—?"

"Everyone has to be a funny man."

A sharp pain exploded in Ash's head. He flew forward with a curse just as everything went black.

23

Deana blew out a deep breath, trying not to worry. She glanced at her watch for the thousandth time. Ash had told her he would be coming to her home as soon as he got off work.

"There's nothing to worry about," she said aloud.

Deana didn't know who she was trying to convince.

The universe or herself.

"He'll be here." She snatched her cell phone from the coffee table and looked at the unanswered text she'd sent him a while ago. She tossed it back and fell onto her couch.

It was close to ten o'clock, and still no word from Ash.

The television was on, but Deana had not been able to keep her focus on it. Grabbing the remote, she flicked though the channels before stopping at the news with the current story snagging her attention.

"Tonight's top story, Columbia Police Department is tackling the war on crime," the male newscaster announced.

Deana's heart skipped a beat. She turned the volume up so she could hear. This was one broadcast she didn't want to miss.

"Yes, they are, Tom. It's good to know the police are seriously trying to make our neighborhoods safe again," the female anchor said. "For years, gang violence has been increasing each year."

Deana had hoped they would speak on anything that may have gone down that Ash would have been involved in. It would have helped her anxiety to at least see him with the help of the news story covering a call the SWAT guys had gone on, but no luck. The story was just general, and a representative from the department was interviewed by the anchors.

She looked down at her phone and didn't know if she should text Sarena or Aspen. They'd probably assure her that this was normal, but at the moment, Deana didn't like the sense of dread that had settled in her stomach.

Something was off.

She didn't know what or why she felt the way she did, but she just had a feeling she didn't like.

Glancing at the papers on her coffee table, she had

a ton of grading to do. That would certainly keep her occupied.

She reached for the papers and her red pen and paused at the sound of her doorbell ringing.

Her heart raced.

Ash.

Finally!

Deana jumped from the couch. She rushed over to the front door but slowed down seeing familiar figures standing out on the porch through the frosted glass.

She flipped the outside light on and flung the door open.

Mac, Declan, and Myles.

"No, no, no, no," she whimpered, shaking her head, leaning against the door. Her eyes became blurry from the tears.

Not Ash.

Please, God. Not Ash.

"May we come in?" Mac asked.

She nodded, unable to speak. She stepped back and waved them in. She bit her lip to keep herself from crying.

Shutting the door, she followed the three men into her living room. They each were dressed in their civilian clothing with badges hanging around their necks.

"Have a seat, Deana," Myles said, motioning

toward the couch.

Declan walked over and shut her television off.

Her heart seemed to be lodged in her throat as she sat. She wiped the tears that burned a trail along her cheeks.

"What's going on?" she demanded.

Be strong, woman.

"Have you heard from Ash?" Declan asked. He stood in front of the television and folded his arms in front of his chest.

"No, not since earlier today before I met Aspen and Sarena for happy hour," she admitted. She eyed the three of them, wanting them to get to the point. "So he's not dead?" she blurted out.

"Not that we know of," Mac replied. He stepped over to her and sat on the coffee table before her. He reached out and took her hand in his.

She was slightly comforted by it. As gruff-natured as he seemed, it was refreshing to see his softer side.

"We don't know exactly what happened, but we found his duffle bag on the ground next to his truck. His phone was found on the street where we are assuming he was loaded into a vehicle."

"He was kidnapped?" She gasped.

"Yes. We reviewed the security footage from the parking lot. He was taken by gunpoint by two men," Declan said.

Her hand flew to her mouth in shock.

Tears streamed down her face. She didn't care if she appeared weak in front of these hardened SWAT guys.

She'd just received news that the love of her life had been taken.

At gunpoint.

"We're going to get him back, Deana," Myles assured her. He came to sit beside her on the couch. He was a large man and had a look of anger to him. She pitied the person who crossed him. Hell, any of them. "There's no way I will sleep without getting him back."

Deana nodded. She glanced around the room and saw the same look of determination on Declan's and Mac's faces.

"Ash trusts you guys with his life," she said. Using the back of her hands, she wiped the tears away. "Do you know who has him?"

"We have a hunch," Mac said, meeting her gaze. "Ash is like a brother to all of us. None of us will rest until we can deliver him back to you safe and sound."

Deana jerked her head in a nod. She believed him, too. She'd seen the way the guys were with each other.

"Is there somewhere you can stay? We're not sure exactly how far these men will go and we'd feel better if you were somewhere safe."

"Ash would have our asses if something happened to you." Myles chuckled.

"He sure would," Declan muttered.

Deana smiled. "I can go over to my friend's house."

Erin wouldn't care if she stayed over with her. Deana reached for her cell phone. It was late, but she was sure Erin would still be awake.

"Why doesn't she stay with Sarena? Mac's house is secure, and we can be sure nothing would happen to her," Myles suggested.

She glanced between the three of them, and they jerked their heads in agreement.

"Good idea. I'll text her now." Mac stood from his perch and moved away.

"Pack a bag, Deana. Looks like there's going to be a slumber party at the MacArthur house." Myles laughed.

She stood from the couch and headed for her bedroom. These were Ash's teammates, and if they wanted her in a safe place, she just do as she was told. She was learning quick to not ask questions.

Ash woke to a throbbing headache. He blinked and found his head covered by a dark cloth. He did a quick assessment of his body and found his arms restrained in front of him. Whoever these fuckers were had left his legs free.

He lay on his side, apparently in the back of a van. They must have knocked him out and thrown him in the back of their vehicle to transport him. Murmurs of deep voices filtered from somewhere.

Apparently, they had no honor.

If he had known they were going to do that, he wouldn't have gone to the van so easily. They would have had to work to get his ass in the back.

Remaining quiet, he strained to hear their conversation.

"House will show these cops that this is his town," one of them said.

Ash bit back a snort.

Viktor Huff didn't know what he had started by kidnapping a cop. His nickname depicting his size meant nothing. He wouldn't know what hit him once Mac and the rest of his team came after him.

Ash knew without a doubt that once SWAT knew he was missing, they would rain hell upon the Demon Lords.

Ash shifted with the motion of the van turning a corner. Without his sight, it appeared his other senses were heightening.

The speed of the vehicle was lowering.

Ash prepared mentally to get himself together. There was no telling what was going to happen to him.

Thoughts of Deana fluttered through his mind, and he cursed leaving while she had been sleeping. She had looked so peaceful in her slumber, and he hadn't had the heart to wake her. She would have been worried out of her mind, and he hadn't wanted to see the fear in her eyes. It would have haunted him while he'd been on the mission.

There was so much he wanted to say to her, but he'd thought they would have much more time.

When he returned to her—and he would— he was going to put everything on the table. He'd make sure that Deana knew she was the only one for him.

The vehicle slowed to a halt.

Ash's muscles tensed at the sounds of the engine shutting off. The doors opened and closed, muffling his captors' voices.

The rattle of the side door opening greeted Ash's ears.

"Rise and shine, princess," one of his captors muttered.

Ash was grabbed and dragged to the edge. His legs were brought to dangle from the van's opening.

"You can stop acting like you're still out. I can tell by the rising and falling of your chest that you're awake," the other one said.

Well, damn. I'm going to have to work on my acting skills.

"It's comforting to know you really care enough to study my breathing patterns." Ash snorted.

A hand gripped his shirt and jerked him to a standing position.

"Shut up."

He was guided along. He stumbled on purpose, giving off the sense that he was unstable walking blind.

But in reality, Ash was trying to get a feel of what and who was around him.

A series of beeps sounding before an alert bleeped.

The security system.

They entered a building with the men guiding him.

Ash memorized each turn and the pathway.

He would need them for later.

"We're here for Mr. Huff," Goon One announced.

The hand on his shoulder tightened and pulled Ash back, signaling for him to stop.

"Is he expecting you?" a female asked haughtily.

"Fuck, Jenny. Let us in," the gangster behind Ash growled. "This is the guy he wants."

"Fine." She sighed. "Go in."

A buzz sounded.

"Let's go, tough guy."

Ash was shoved from behind. His irritation grew

from the manhandling. The gangsters though they were macho and hard. Ash ground his teeth.

"Mr. Huff. We have the cop you wanted," Goon Two stated.

The dressing was removed from Ash's head. He blinked several times before his vision cleared, allowing him to glance around the room quickly to take in his surroundings.

Ash recognized they were in an abandoned building by the looks of the area outside the window. Only this one had upgrades. The office was moderated and could almost be deemed masculine elegance for a businessman.

His gaze landed on an impressively sized man behind a desk.

Viktor Huff, also known as House.

The nickname certainly fit him.

Ash held his gaze, refusing to back down.

"Officer Ashton Fraser," Viktor's deep baritone voice cut through the tense silence.

"Viktor Huff," Ash replied. His escorts were standing on each side of him. "If you wanted a meeting with me, a call to schedule one would have sufficed."

Viktor's lip curled up in the corner. He pushed back his chair and stood to his full height. He buttoned his dark suit jacket and walked around the desk.

"You and the Columbia police department have

been busy," Viktor snapped.

"Well, there's a lot of scum to clean up in this city." Ash glanced at the men standing on each side of him before turning his attention back to Viktor.

"You and your men have cost me a lot of money."

Ash held back a smile.

Good.

Hitting the gangster where it would hurt the most was the first step.

"I hope you have an insurance policy out on everything we've confiscated." Ash chuckled.

Viktor stepped toward Ash and stood before him. His unwavering gaze was locked on Ash. His attempt to intimidate him failed.

"Half a million dollars is no laughing matter, Officer Fraser," Viktor sneered, ramming his finger into Ash's chest. "Someone is going to pay me back my money or it's going to be your ass on the line."

Ash grew solemn.

Fuck.

"I see you understand I'm serious." Viktor shoved Ash, sending him falling backwards. His two goons caught him and righted him. "I'd hate to see something happen to your pretty little schoolteacher."

Red clouded Ash's vision. Threats to Deana sent him to a dark place he'd never wanted to visit. He would do anything necessary to keep her safe.

Ash shook them off him, but their grips tightened on his arms.

"You lay one hand on her, and I swear I will—"

"You're in no position to make threats, Officer Fraser." Viktor folded his massive arms against his chest.

"You think my men will back down if you take me out?" Ash snapped. He balled his hands up into fists. How he wished these handcuffs were off. "Kill me, and I promise you cops will be so far up your ass, even God above won't be able to pull them out. Mac won't rest until you are in a jail cell—"

"The police won't be able to stop me," Viktor yelled. He flew forward and snatched Ash up by the neck of his shirt. "This is my fucking town. I will go through every man in blue if I have to."

An alarm sounded behind Viktor's desk. He paused and stalked over there with a curse.

Ash's gaze followed him to a bank of monitors that were currently filled with white snow.

"What the hell is going on?" Viktor pulled a gun from inside his jacket.

Ash began to chuckle. It started from deep within him and spilled out. He shook his head while glancing from Goon One and Two before turning his attention to Viktor.

"You sure this is your town?" He cocked an eyebrow at Viktor.

24

"Hank. Black. Go find out what the hell is going on out there," Viktor commanded.

The men turned and stormed out of the room. Viktor walked back over to Ash with the barrel of his gun pointed at him.

Ash's muscles grew tense watching Viktor get close to him. His fists were bunched tight in anticipation. The desire to slam his fist in the gangster's face was strong.

"Lost a half a million dollars in profit, and tonight's not going your way. Now that's just fucked up." Ash gave a low, dry chuckle.

"I'm getting sick and tired of your lame-ass jokes," Viktor snapped. He drew back his weapon and pointed it at Ash.

Ash swiftly ducked and swung his arms. His fist knocked Viktor's gun away. It scattered along the floor, far from them.

With a yell, Viktor threw a fist. It connected with Ash's solar plexus.

Ash released a grunt but refused to go down. He swung his bound wrists and landed a swift punch to Viktor's chin. The gangster flew back and landed on the floor. Pain exploded in Ash's hands, but he ignored it.

There was no way he would let Viktor get the upper hand over him.

Handcuffed or not.

Ash ran over to Viktor. He drew his leg back with a yell and kicked with all his might. Viktor's body writhed on the floor. Ash landed another one, using as much of his strength as he could.

Viktor rolled away from Ash. Lights reflected off a dark metal object not too far away.

The gun.

Ash's gaze landed on it then flickered back to Viktor. Ash dashed forward while Viktor scrambled to it. Ash jumped and landed on top of him. He swung his hands over Viktor's head, pulling the handcuffs back against Viktor's throat.

Shouting and the sounds of gunfire rattled outside the office door.

Ash wrestled with Viktor who was still reaching for the gun. Ash pulled back harder, trying to prevent Viktor's hand from reaching it.

Viktor's hands came up and clawed up at the chain pressing against his neck.

"You'll go through every man in blue, huh?" Ash growled. Ignoring the burning around his wrist, he tugged harder. The sounds of Viktor's strangled gasps filled the air. "You'll first have to go through me."

Hands grabbed Ash from Viktor and threw him to the floor.

"Mr. Huff," Henry shouted, rolling Viktor over who was gasping for breath. "We have to go. It's the cops. They are swarming the building."

Black dragged Ash away from his boss before landing a swift kick to his side. Ash groaned, staggering away.

"Where the hell are you going?" Black bellowed. He snatched Ash up from the floor. "Grab Mr. Huff. We need to leave. Now."

"You're not going anywhere," a familiar voice countered from behind them.

Declan.

Black jerked around with Ash who swayed on his feet.

Ash's gaze landed on the three men in black fatigues that stood with their guns aimed at the gangbangers.

Their stares were fierce and feral.

His brothers in blue.

"CPD. Don't fucking move, or I will shoot you in the face," Mac growled.

Black's hand disappeared from Ash's shoulder.

"You better do what he says," Myles scoffed. "Or you'll be leaving here in a body bag."

"Throw down your weapons and kneel on the floor with your hands collapsed behind your head." Declan's voice was ice-cold hard.

Ash turned slightly and watched with satisfaction Viktor and his men comply.

The rest of the SWAT team entered the room and went straight to Viktor and his men, placing them in zip ties.

Ash teetered on his feet and met the gazes of his team.

"About fucking time," he muttered. His knees no longer had the strength to hold him up. He fell to the floor, but arms caught him, keeping him from slamming onto the ground face-first.

"Gotcha," Myles murmured.

"What took you fuckers so long?" Ash grumbled.

"We made a pit stop by Deana's and moved her. We didn't want to take any chances they'd come after her," Myles explained.

Police officers swarmed the room, taking Viktor and his men into custody.

Myles helped Ash to his feet.

Viktor threw Ash a frosty glare as he was led out of the room. Ash's gaze dropped down to the angry dark marks along the gangster's neck.

"Let's get these cuffs off you and get you to the hospital," Declan said, coming up with a set of keys in his hands.

Ash held out his arms. He shook his head. "No hospital."

He needed to get to Deana and make sure she was safe and sound.

"It was not a request, Ash," Mac barked.

Ash winced, knowing he was not in the mood to argue with Mac.

The cuffs fell to the floor. Ash immediately massaged where the skin was rubbed raw. Visions of Deana came to mind, and the need to be with her filled him.

"I'm fine, Mac," Ash assured him, but Mac's face was rock-hard.

"I'm not going to repeat myself, Fraser. It's an order. Go willingly, or I'll put those cuffs back on you myself and drag you."

Ash glanced around the room and saw the determined look on each of his teammates' faces. None of them would stop Mac. Letting out an audible sigh, he rolled his eyes.

"Fine. I'll get checked out, and then that's it."

"I wonder which of them will be next," Sarena remarked, sitting back on her couch.

Deana took a sip of her wine while her curiosity grew. "What do you mean?"

The guys had brought her to Mac's home where Sarena had been waiting with snacks and wine. Dressed in pajamas, they both lounged around in the living room, ignoring the movie playing on the television.

It was the adult version of a slumber party, only they were waiting to hear if the guys had found Ash or not. No matter how much Sarena tried to distract her, it didn't work.

She appreciated everything they were doing for her, but until Ash was back in her arms, it would be hard for her to completely relax.

"Well, if you haven't noticed, the guys have been very anti-relationship. They have some weird notion that being SWAT, it would be hard to love them," Sarena replied, draining her glass.

"Really? Like, as if they are supposed to be alone forever?" Deana glanced down at her glass, remembering the first time she'd laid eyes on Ash. She'd never got the lone wolf feel from him.

"Yup. Loving a SWAT guy is hard, I was told."

Sarena giggled. "I don't think it's so much the job half the time, more that it's their stubborn, macho attitudes."

Deana chuckled. Ash could be stubborn, but she never had to question his feelings for her.

"They actually said that?" Deana raised her eyebrow.

"Not in so many ways. Mac was against the whole relationship vibe. When we first got together, I had just moved next door to him, and we sort of 'hooked up'."

Deana's eyes grew wide. "Are you serious?"

"Yup." Sarena leaned forward and grabbed the wine bottle, refilling her glass. She tipped the bottle to Deana.

She knew she shouldn't drink too much.

Ash may need her.

Her gaze fell back to the bottle, and she shrugged.

When in Rome.

She held her glass out and allowed Sarena to top her off.

"That's wild." Deana sat back in amazement.

"Marcas had this whole non-dating clause. But, of course, he couldn't resist all this." Sarena giggled, waving her hand along her body.

Deana burst out in laughter.

If it wasn't for Sarena, Deana didn't know what she

would have done. She would probably be just sitting by the phone, anxiously waiting for it to ring.

"Okay, so you and Mac got together first, then Declan and Aspen. Who do you think is next?" Deana asked, joining the game. Ash's team was a great group of men. They all deserved what she and Ash had.

"Well, let's see. Iker just broke up with his short-lived girlfriend, Zain's wife left him a few years ago, and from what I know, he's just a one-night stand man now." Sarena tapped her fingers to her chin, lost in thought. "Brodie, hmmm... I could see him falling hard for someone. He has a big heart, and Myles...he's a big old flirt, and whoever catches his eye better be able to handle him."

Deana jumped at the sound of a phone ringing. She finished off her wine and set the glass on the table while Sarena answered her phone. She was going to ignore the simple fact that Sarena had just filled it and it was already empty.

She'd blame it on her nerves.

Wine solved almost everything.

Deana would have to admit she was a little disappointed that it wasn't her phone that had rung. She openly listened to Sarena's side of the conversation in hopes of news of Ash.

"Hello? Marcas!" Sarena's gaze connected with Deana's. Her heart raced while she waited for what she prayed was good news. "We're fine. Just having a glass of wine." She paused, a small smile crossing her face. "Don't worry about how many glasses of wine. A situation like this causes for something harder, but it's all I had in the house." The smile on her lips slowly faded.

Deana was dying to know what Mac was saying.

She bit her lip and leaned forward, resting her feet on the floor.

"Did they find him?" Deana whispered, unable to contain her anxiety any longer.

Sarena nodded, and relief filled her.

"Okay, Marcas. I'll let her know. Come home soon, babe," Sarena said before hanging up. She tossed the phone to the couch with a sigh. "They have him. They're en route to the hospital."

"The hospital!" Deana cried out. Her vision blurred with tears at the thought of Ash being harmed.

"It's not bad. Just their standard precautions. According to Marcas, he was forcing Ash to go get checked out at the hospital," Sarena said reassuringly.

Deana nodded and beat down the wave of fear that coursed through her body.

"Do we know which one?" Deana asked, getting to her feet. There was no way she could just sit and wait for him. Now that he was out of danger, she needed to see him. Hold him. Kiss him. Tell him how much she loved him.

"Sure do." Sarena jumped up from her seat. She grabbed the remote and turned off the television. "They are taking him to my job."

"I have to go to him," Deana said. She'd have to find a way up to the hospital.

"You sure do. Go get dressed," Sarena ordered, apparently knowing exactly what Deana was thinking. She walked over and pushed Deana toward the stairs. "I'm calling for an Uber."

25

"Don't you dare move," a voice ordered from the doorway.

Ash paused on the edge of the bed and glanced up to see who dared bark commands at him.

Ronnie, Sarena's best friend.

Ash didn't know her well, but if she was a friend of Sarena's then she was a friend of his. They'd been at a few gatherings together, and she seemed sweet. Ash had never been alone with her until today.

"You don't get to tell me what to do," he muttered, placing his feet on the floor.

"I'm just the messenger, compliments of Mac," she said haughtily. Pushing off the doorjamb, she walked into the room, ignoring his hard stare. "Let me take your blood pressure."

"I'm fine," he stressed, but she ignored him again.

She grabbed the cuff and stood beside the bed, waiting.

Yes, she's definitely friends with Sarena.

Mac's stubbornness must be rubbing off on his wife and her friend.

"Just give me your arm. Please."

Running a hand along his face, Ash decided he'd better choose his battles wisely. He didn't want to chance her running off to Mac to tattle on him.

"Fine." He held out his arm.

She wrapped the device around it and hit a button on a monitor. His arm began to be compressed while the machine did its job.

"I need to use a phone—"

"Shh..." she said, putting her finger to her lips.

Ash rolled his eyes. He was fine. Why couldn't they just believe him? He'd been in the emergency room for under an hour, had seen the doctors once, had a few X-rays, and had his wrist cleaned and bandaged.

He was practically good as new.

"Okay. Perfect," she quipped when a beeping noise sounded. The cuff around his arm relaxed, allowing her to remove it.

"Told you so," he mumbled with a roll of his eyes. "I need a phone. Do you have one I can use?"

"My cell is locked up in my locker, but I guess I can take you to one." She waved for him to follow her.

"About time." He sighed, standing. He walked out

into the hallway of the busy nursing unit and glanced around.

Brodie leaned against the reception desk, openly flirting with a young woman in scrubs. Iker and Zain were at the end of the hall talking amongst themselves.

Ash shook his head and turned his attention back to Ronnie.

No sign of Mac.

Good.

"There's one on the wall over there. Just hit nine first to get an outside line." Ronnie pointed in the direction down the hall.

"Thanks, Ronnie."

"Stubborn cops," she muttered, striding away with a shake of her head.

Ash chuckled and headed toward the phone. Ronnie just didn't know how stubborn he could be. Arriving at the phone, he picked it up and dialed Deana's number. She would be worried with the news of his capture.

He needed to hear her voice.

He needed to see her.

Hell, he needed to feel her in his arms again.

Everything would be okay.

He placed the receiver to his ear. It rang and rang before her voicemail came on.

Hi. You've reached Deana. I'm not available now.

Please feel free to leave a message, and I'll get back to you as soon as I can. Bye.

Ash closed his eyes and leaned his forearm against the wall, unsure what to say.

"Hey, babe. It's me..." His voice trailed off. What should he say?

I'm not a captive?

I'm at the hospital?

"It's me," he began, closing his eyes. His voice caught in his throat. Emotions he'd never really experienced before filled his chest. "Deana, there's so much I want to say to you. I can't wait to—"

"Tell me now," a small voice said behind him.

He swung around to see Deana standing there with tears spilling down her face.

He ignored Mac, Sarena, and the rest of his team standing back watching them.

His focus was on Deana.

She was dressed in a t-shirt and leggings. Her red ringlets were left free in their natural state.

She was his world and all that mattered.

The phone slid from his hand. He stepped forward and opened his arms. With a cry, Deana flew toward him and slammed into his body.

A grunt escaped him, and he wrapped his arms around her, pressing a kiss to the top of her head while she buried her face in his chest as her body was racked with sobs.

"I love you so much," he breathed. He couldn't let her go if he tried.

"I love you, too," she replied, tilting her head back. Her lips curved up into a smile. It faltered while she stared into his eyes. "I tried to be strong, Ash. I did, but I couldn't help but be worried about you—"

He cut her off by covering her lips with his. Deana's lips instantly parted, allowing him to thoroughly kiss her. She collapsed her hands together at the base of his neck and returned the kiss with the same fever he had for her.

Cheers and claps sounded behind them, but all Ash wanted to hear was that Deana loved him.

"Say it again," he murmured, his lips brushing hers. He gently cupped her face in his hands, running his thumb along her cheek, following the path of her tears. He didn't like seeing her worry, and there was nothing more he wanted to do but to take her home and show her how much he needed her.

"I love you, Ashton Fraser. Please tell me you're okay," she breathed.

Her gaze dropped down to his wrists. Her eyes widened, and he instantly tipped her chin up to take her attention from the bandages.

"I am now. Nothing will keep me from returning to you," he promised.

"You promise?" she asked, studying his face.

"With every breath I take. I'll always come back to you."

EPILOGUE

"Oh my. This food is so good," Deana gushed. She grabbed her rib and took another bite.

"I told you Mac was a master on the grill." Ash laughed at her enthusiastically chewing.

Lately, Deana hadn't had an appetite much, but today, it returned to her with full gusto.

"I need him to invite us over at least twice a week," she muttered.

Today was the quarterly cookout that was held at Mac and Sarena's. It was a beautiful day for the team to gather together, relax, eat good food, and bond.

Sitting in the shade, there was a slight chill in the air. She pulled her thin jacket closed and took in the guys all having a good time.

A couple of the guys had been tossing a football around in the back yard until Mac had announced it was time to eat.

Now the team was spread out on the deck enjoying the feast.

"So as I was saying," Myles's boisterous voice echoed around them. "We rush in the room, and there is Ash looking like he'd been run over by a bull."

"Hey." Ash laughed. He wiped his hands on a napkin before tossing it at Myles. "Before ya'll got there, I had everything under control."

Deana pushed down her anxiety at hearing a replay of a night she wanted to erase from her memory. She didn't want to remember how scared she had been thinking that Ash would never return to her.

"Sure you did." Declan chuckled, tipping his beer bottle toward Ash. "We all believe you."

Snickers went around.

"Wait a minute," Deana said. She'd just realized something that hadn't been explained to her. She took a sip of her sweet tea and placed her glass back down on the table. "How did you guys know where he was?"

That had never been told.

"She's right. How did you guys know?" Aspen asked.

"Well, Brodie here," Ash began, tipping his beer to his team member, "has a college buddy who apparently is a technology mogul who had been working with a few government agencies and trackers. He had been wanting to work with the local police departments on some things he was trialing and sent them over to Brodie."

"Theo gave me three bracelets that had microchips implanted in them. They have world-wide GPS tracking in them, so no matter where the person is who is wearing it, they can be found," Brodie said.

"Wow. That's something you hear of in movies." Sarena chuckled.

"The department is looking into using it for our narcotics officers who go under deep cover," Mac announced.

Deana sighed and leaned against Ash. Her gaze dropped down to her empty plate. She was full, but there was a pecan cobbler sitting over on the food table that was calling her.

"You all right?" Ash murmured, laying a kiss on her forehead. He ran a hand along her back.

"Yeah. I'll be right back." She stood from the table and took her jacket off. Her gaze met Ash's.

His lips curled into a wide grin.

Conversation around them came to a halt.

Deana innocently looked around at the group.

All eyes were on her.

"Since we have you all together," Ash began, standing from his seat. He grabbed Deana's hand and entwined their fingers. "We wanted to tell you all at the same time."

Deana ran a hand along the slight swell of her belly with a smile. "We're expecting!"

The patio exploded with laughter, cheers, and applause. Deana turned to Ash with an abundance of love for him. She reached up and cupped his jaw.

I love you, she mouthed.

He tossed her a wink and pressed a quick kiss to her lips right before they were bombarded by their friends.

Her gaze was captured by the reflection of the sun on her massive diamond ring on her hand.

Her life was perfect, and she couldn't ask for anything more.

Love what you've just read?
More SWAT action will be on the way!

A NOTE FROM THE AUTHOR

Dear reader,

Thank you for taking the time to read Dirty Operations. I hope you enjoyed Ash and Deana's story! If you want more from the Special Weapons & Tactics series, then please leave a short review on the platform you purchased this book on. It doesn't matter how long or how short, ALL REVIEWS MATTER!

Warm wishes,
Peyton Banks

ABOUT THE AUTHOR

Peyton Banks is the alter ego of a city girl who is a romantic at heart. Her mornings consist of coffee and daydreaming up the next steamy romance book ideas. She loves spinning romantic tales of hot alpha males and the women they love. Make sure you check her out!

Sign up for Peyton's Newsletter to find out the latest releases, giveaways and news! Click HERE to sign up!

Want to know the latest about Peyton Banks? Follow her online

ALSO BY PEYTON BANKS

Current Free Short Story

Summer Escape

Special Weapons & Tactics Series

Dirty Tactics (Special Weapons & Tactics 1)

Dirty Ballistics (Special Weapons & Tactics 2)

Dirty Operations (Special Weapons & Tactics 3)

Dirty Alliance (Special Weapons & Tactics 4) TBD

Interracial Romances (BWWM)

Pieces of Me

Hard Love

Retain Me

Obsessive Temptation: A BWWM Romance Limited Edition Collection

Emerging Temptation: A BWWM Romance Limited Edition Collection (Coming Soon)

Mafia Romance Series

Unexpected Allies (The Tokhan Bratva 1)

Unexpected Chaos (The Tokhan Bratva 2) TBD

Unexpected Hero (The Tokhan Bratva 3) TBD